June's menu
BARONESSA GELATERIA
in Boston's North End

In addition to our regular flavors of
Italian gelato, this month we are featuring:

- **Puffy clouds of fresh-whipped meringue**

  Nothing excited Alex Barone more than flying
  the skies for his country in his supercharged
  navy jet with the Blue Angels. Close second?
  A beautiful woman waiting for him on land.
  After all, he didn't get the nickname "Babe
  Magnet Barone" for nothing....

- **Red, white and blue torte**

  A Barone heir and a waitress? Daisy knew
  it was an insane combination. Sooner or
  later the red-blooded Boston blue blood
  Alex Barone would come to his senses.
  Until then, she'd simply savor their white-hot
  attraction....

- **An array of decadent desserts**

  After being so long denied, Alex and Daisy,
  friends by day, became lovers in the night.
  Their hands, their mouths, took them on a
  sensual journey of discovery. Then Alex
  took command—and brought Daisy to new
  heights of passion....

  Buon appetito!

Dear Reader,

Top off your summer reading list with six brand-new steamy romances from Silhouette Desire!

Reader favorite Ann Major brings the glamorous LONE STAR COUNTRY CLUB miniseries into Desire with *Shameless* (#1513). This rancher's reunion romance is the first of three titles set in Mission Creek, Texas—where society reigns supreme and appearances are everything. Next, our exciting yearlong series DYNASTIES: THE BARONES continues with *Beauty & the Blue Angel* (#1514) by Maureen Child, in which a dashing naval hero goes overboard for a struggling mom-to-be.

Princess in His Bed (#1515) by *USA TODAY* bestselling author Leanne Banks is the third Desire title in her popular miniseries THE ROYAL DUMONTS. Enjoy the fun as a tough Wyoming rancher loses his heart to a spirited royal-in-disguise. Next, a brooding horseman shows a beautiful rancher the ropes…of desire in *The Gentrys: Abby* (#1516) by Linda Conrad.

In the latest BABY BANK title, *Marooned with a Millionaire* (#1517) by Kristi Gold, passion ignites between a powerful hotel magnate and the pregnant balloonist stranded on his yacht. And a millionaire M.D. brings out the temptress in his tough-girl bodyguard in *Sleeping with the Playboy* (#1518) by veteran Harlequin Historicals and debut Desire author Julianne MacLean.

Get your summer off to a sizzling start with six new passionate, powerful and provocative love stories from Silhouette Desire.

Enjoy!

Melissa Jeglinski
Senior Editor, Silhouette Desire

Please address questions and book requests to:
Silhouette Reader Service
U.S.: 3010 Walden Ave., P.O. Box 1325, Buffalo, NY 14269
Canadian: P.O. Box 609, Fort Erie, Ont. L2A 5X3

Beauty & the
Blue Angel
MAUREEN CHILD

Silhouette®

Desire®

Published by Silhouette Books
America's Publisher of Contemporary Romance

Special thanks and acknowledgment are given to Maureen Child for her contribution to the DYNASTIES: THE BARONES series.

 SILHOUETTE BOOKS

ISBN 0-373-76514-2

BEAUTY & THE BLUE ANGEL

Visit Silhouette at www.eHarlequin.com

Printed in U.S.A.

Books by Maureen Child

MAUREEN CHILD

is a California native who loves to travel. Every chance they get, she and her husband are taking off on another research trip. The author of more than sixty books, Maureen loves a happy ending and still swears that she has the best job in the world. She lives in Southern California with her husband, two children and a golden retriever with delusions of grandeur.

Visit her Web site at www.maureenchild.com.

DYNASTIES: THE BARONES

Meet the Barones of Boston—an elite clan caught in a web of danger, deceit…and desire!

Alex Barone—The one time he let his heart take the pilot seat, it got broken. His fiancée jilted him on Valentine's Day—shade of the Barone curse. Alex prefers the fast life in the Blue Angels, flying all around the world. He's not looking for a white picket fence to hold him in….

Daisy Cusak—The minute she told her ex-boyfriend she was pregnant, he left her in a cloud of dust. Daisy's prepared to be both mother *and* father to her baby now; she'll do whatever it takes. She's not looking for a love-'em-and-leave-'em flyboy….

Rita Barone—Alex's sister, a nurse, delivers Daisy's healthy, perfect little girl. Now she's interested in delivering another Barone to the altar.

One

Daisy Cusak ignored the ribbon of pain snaking through her. "Just a twinge," she whispered, then ran the palm of her hand across her swollen belly. "Come on, sweetie, don't do this to Mommy, okay?"

The pains had been intermittent all day, but she'd brushed them off. All of the books said there was nothing to worry about until the contractions were steady and just a few minutes apart. Well, heck. One every hour and a half or so wasn't anything to worry about, right?

Besides, on a busy Friday night, she could make a lot of tips serving dinner at Antonio's Italian restaurant. And right now, that money would mean a lot.

All around her, noises of the busy kitchen echoed—pans clashing, chefs cursing, expensive china plates clinking. It was music of a sort. And the waiters and waitresses were the dancers.

She'd been doing this for four years and she was darn good at it. Though people wouldn't exactly consider being a waitress a career, Daisy didn't have a problem with it. She loved her job. She met new people every night, had a few regulars who would wait an extra half hour just to get seated in her station, and her bosses, the Contis, were just so darn nice to work for.

Rather than fire her for being pregnant, members of the Conti family were continually urging her to sit down, get off her feet. Someone was always near to help her with the heavier trays, and she'd already been assured that her job would be waiting for her after she took some time off with the baby.

"You'll see," she said, smiling down at her unborn child. "It's going to be great. *We're* going to be great."

"Everything all right, Daisy?"

She turned abruptly and grinned at Joan, one of the other waitresses. "Sure. I'm good."

The other woman looked as though she didn't believe her, and Daisy silently wished she was just a little bit better at lying.

"Why don't you take a break?" Joan said. "I'll cover your tables for you."

"It's okay," Daisy answered firmly, willing not only Joan, but herself, to believe it. "I'm fine. Honest."

Her friend gave her a worried frown, then stacked two plates of veal parmigiana on her serving tray. "Okay, but I've got my eye on you."

Along with everyone else at Antonio's, Daisy thought. She picked up a pot of coffee, pushed through the Out door and walked into the main dining room. Casual elegance flavored the room. Snowy-white linens draped the tables, candles flickered wildly within the crystal hurricane globes and soft strains of weeping violin music drifted from the overhead speakers.

Above the music came the comfortable murmur of voices, punctuated every once in a while by someone's laughter. Wineglasses clinked, forks and knives clattered against china, and men and women dressed in starched white shirts and creased black trousers moved through the crowd with choreographed precision.

Daisy smiled at her customers as she offered more coffee and took orders. She bent to grin at a toddler who was strapped into his high chair and laughing over the spaghetti he'd rubbed into his hair. Most of the wait staff hated having kids in their sections. It usually meant lost time when the customers left, because the mess had to be cleaned before anyone else could be seated. And lost time meant lost money.

But Daisy had always loved kids. Even the messy, cranky ones. Which, Joan had told her too many times to count, made Daisy nuts.

A group of men in their thirties followed the hostess and began to thread their way through the maze of tables to the huge, dark maroon leather booth at the back of Daisy's station. As they passed, she caught a look of apology from the hostess seating them. Four men would be big eaters and probably end up running Daisy's legs off. On the bright side, though, they might turn out to be good tippers, too. And she was always trying to beef up the nest egg building ever so slowly in the bank.

Another pain gripped her, this time sharply, briefly, in the middle of her back, and Daisy stiffened in reaction. Oh no, honey. Not now.

As if her baby heard that silent plea, the pain drifted away into nothing more than a slow, nagging ache. That Daisy could handle.

All she had to do was get through the next couple of hours and she'd be home free.

All he had to do was get through the next couple of hours and he'd be home free. That was what Alex Barone kept telling himself.

He was the last to be seated, and caught himself damn near perched on the edge of the leather banquette, as if ready to hit the floor running. When that thought flashed through his mind, he gritted his teeth and eased back on the bench seat. Damned if he'd feel guilty for coming into this restaurant.

Damned if he'd worry about the ramifications.

Although, if he'd known his friends were going to choose Antonio's, he might have bowed out. There was no point in going out of his way to antagonize an old family enemy.

He glanced around at the place and smiled to himself. As a Barone, he'd been raised with stories that made the Conti family sound like demons. But if this was their hell, they'd made a nice place of it. Dim lighting, soft music…the scents coming out of the kitchen nearly made him groan in appreciation.

Nearly every table was full, and the wait staff looked busy as ground troops settling in for a big campaign. That thought brought a smile. He'd been in the military too long.

While his friends laughed and talked, Alex let his gaze drift around the room again, keeping a watchful eye out for any loose Contis. But since none of them knew Alex personally, what were the chances he'd be recognized as a Barone? Slim to none.

So he was just going to relax, have dinner, then leave with no one the wiser.

In the next instant, all thoughts of leaving raced from his brain.

"Hello, my name is Daisy and I'll be your server tonight."

A gorgeous woman seemed to appear out of nowhere, standing right beside Alex as she gave the whole table a smile wide and bright enough to light up all the shadowy corners in the room.

A purely male instinct had Alex straightening up in his seat for a closer, more thorough look. Her long, curly chestnut hair was caught at the nape of her neck with a slightly tarnished silver barrette. Her eyes weren't quite blue or green, but a tantalizing combination of both. Her pale skin looked satin smooth and soft. Her voice held just a hint of humor. Alex's interest was piqued…until her enormous belly nearly bumped him as she shifted position on what had to be tired feet.

Pregnant.

Taken.

Well, damn. Disappointment shot through him. His gaze dropped automatically to her ring finger. Nothing. Not even a white mark to indicate there might have been one there at some point.

He frowned to himself. Not married? What kind of moron would walk away from a woman like this? Especially if she was carrying his child?

"Hello, Daisy," one of the guys—Mike Hannigan—said with a slow whistle of approval.

Alex shot him a disgusted look, but apparently it didn't bother the woman at all.

"Can I start you out with some drinks? Appetizers?" she asked as she handed around several long menus.

"Beers all around," Nick Santee ordered, and she nodded as she made a note on her order pad.

"Your phone number?" Tim Hawkins ventured.

She grinned, and the full, megawatt force of that smile hit Alex like a fist to the gut. Damn, this was one potent female, even in her condition.

"Sure," she said, rubbing one hand along her belly. "It's one eight hundred *way* too pregnant."

Then she turned and walked off to get their drinks. While the guys laughed and kidded Tim about his lousy pickup skills, Alex half turned in his seat to follow her progress through the restaurant. She had a bounce in her step that he liked. The smile on her face had wavered only once, when she'd grimaced and dropped a hand to her belly, as if comforting the child within.

And who, he wondered, comforted *her?*

As the evening wore on, his interest in her only sharpened. When she brought the pitcher of beer and four glasses, he slid out of the booth to take the heavy tray from her.

"Oh. I'm okay, really."

"Never said you weren't, ma'am."

She looked up at him, and he decided that her eyes were more blue than green.

"It's Daisy. Just Daisy."

He nodded, standing there, holding a trayful of drinks and looking down into fathomless eyes that seemed to draw him deeper with every passing second. "I'm Alex."

She licked her lips, pulled in a shuddering breath and let it out again. "Well, thanks for the help...Alex."

"No problem."

He unloaded the beers, handed her back the empty tray and then stood in the aisle watching her walk away.

"Hey, Barone," Nick called, and Alex flinched, hoping no one else had heard his last name.

"What?"

One of the guys laughed.

Nick said, "You gonna sit down and have a beer, or do you want to go on back to the kitchen and help her out there, too?"

Embarrassed to be caught fantasizing about a pregnant woman, Alex grinned and took his seat. Reaching for his beer, he took a long drink, hoping the icy brew would help stamp out the fires within.

But still he couldn't help watching her. She should be tired. Yet her energy never seemed to flag. And she was stronger than her fragile build seemed to indicate. She lifted heavy trays with ease and kept up such a fast pace he was pretty sure if she'd been walking in a straight line, she'd have made it to Cleveland by now.

"Geez, Barone," Nick muttered, leaning closer. "Get a grip. There's lots of pretty women in Boston. Do you have to home in on one who's obviously taken?"

"Who's homing in?" Alex countered. Silently, though, he reminded himself that she wasn't taken. At least not by a man who appreciated her enough to marry her. "I'm just—"

"Window shopping?" Tim asked.

"Close your hole," Mike told him.

Alex glanced around at the men gathered at the table. Men he'd known for years. Like him, they were navy pilots, guys he'd trained with, studied with and flown with. There was a bond between them that even family couldn't match.

And yet...right now, he wished them all to the Antarctic.

Stupid, but he wanted their waitress to himself.

When she set their check on the edge of the table, Alex picked it up quickly, his fingertips brushing hers. She drew back fast, almost as if she'd felt the same snap of electricity he had. Which was kind of weird. She was pregnant, for Pete's sake. Very pregnant. It should have put her off-limits.

"So, are you guys shipping out now?" Daisy asked, trying to keep her gaze from drifting toward the man sitting so close to her.

His friends were easier to deal with. They were friendly, charming, casually flirtatious, like most of the navy men she'd waited on at Antonio's. And she'd treated them as she did all of her customers—with polite friendliness and nothing more.

Since the day Jeff had called her a mantrap and walked out the door, leaving behind not only her but his unborn child, Daisy hadn't given any man a second look. Until tonight. This one—Alex, with the ebony hair and dark brown eyes and sharp-as-a-razor cheekbones—was different. She'd known it the minute he looked at her. And the feeling had only grown over the last hour and a half.

She'd felt his gaze on her most of the night, and didn't even want to think about the feelings that dark, steady stare engendered.

Hormones.

That had to be the reason.

Her hormones were out of whack because of the baby.

"No," Alex said, and she steeled herself to meet that gaze head-on. "We're on leave, actually."

"Are you from Boston?" she asked and told herself she was only being friendly, just as she would with any other customer. But even she didn't believe it.

There was just something about this man...

"I was raised here," he was saying.

One of the other men spoke up, but his voice was like a buzz in her ears. All she heard, all she could see was this man watching her through the darkest, warmest eyes she'd ever seen.

"You have family here?"

A slow, wicked smile curved one side of his mouth, and her stomach jittered. "Yeah, I come from a big family. I'm the fifth of eight kids."

She dropped one hand to the mound of her belly. "Eight. That must be nice."

"Not when I was a kid," he admitted. "Too many people fighting over the TV and cookies."

Daisy smiled at the mental image of a houseful of children, laughing, happy. Then, sadly, she let it go. It was something she'd never known, and now her baby, too, would grow up alone.

No. Not alone. Her baby would always have *her*.

Alex's friends eased out of the booth and headed for the front of the restaurant. He watched them go, nodded, then reached into his wallet for a few bills. He handed her the money and the check and said, "Keep the change."

"Thanks. I mean—" He was leaving. Probably just as well, she told herself. And yet she felt oddly reluctant to let him walk away.

"What are you doing in my restaurant?"

Daisy spun around to watch in amazement as Salvatore Conti, her boss, came rushing out of the kitchen, flapping a pristine white dish towel like some crazed matador looking for a bull.

Two

"**D**amn it." Alex stiffened and braced for a confrontation. He'd hoped to make it out of Antonio's without incident. But it looked as if Sal had other plans.

The older man hurried toward him, still shouting, mindless of the other customers or his employees' fascinated attention. Sal Conti was sixty-two, but he was still pretty spry. About five feet eleven inches tall, he was a little shorter than Alex, and slender. His brown eyes were flashing and his cheeks were filled with furious color.

"What are you doing here?" Sal demanded. "Spying? This is what the Barones have come to now?"

Okay, fine. Alex hadn't wanted a scene, but he'd be damned if he'd stand here and let his family be insulted.

"Spying?" he retorted, standing his ground. "Are all of you Contis paranoid? Or is it just you?"

"Paranoid?" Sal waved that towel furiously, shaking his other fist in the air. "You can talk of paranoid? After what your family's done to mine?"

"What *we've* done? You know damn well it was the Contis behind that gelato fiasco."

"Ridiculous," Sal snapped.

"And as long as we're at it," Alex added, meeting the older man's narrowed gaze with a glare of his own, "I still think your family was behind the arson."

Sal huffed in a breath until his narrow chest swelled. "Slander." He shot a quick look around at his customers and waved that towel again. "You all heard him. That's slander. The Contis were cleared by the police. That's a vicious lie the Barones toss around to make us look bad."

Alex snorted in laughter. "Believe it or not, we don't sit around thinking about the Contis. Besides, you do a great job of looking bad all on your own."

"The Contis have done nothing. We don't need to bring bad fortune onto the Barones." He waved a hand toward the ceiling and the night sky beyond. "It's in the stars. You're all ill-fated."

Ill-fated. Bad fortune. This whole Italian curse

thing had been rattling around between their two families for years, and Alex, for one, was tired of it.

"No such thing as fate," he said.

"Sal…" Daisy moved toward her boss. Taking his arm, she gave it a tug, as if she was used to dealing with the older man's flash temper. Which, Alex thought, she probably was.

But Sal shook her off, and Daisy sighed.

"Stay out of this, Daisy," Alex muttered, and took her arm to pull her back beside him.

Sal noticed the move and his features darkened with fury. "You leave her alone. She's a nice girl and she doesn't need a Barone in her life."

"You're nuts, you know that?" Alex retorted. Hell, for that matter, so was *he*. He was standing here having a shouting match with a man more than twice his age. Swiping one hand across his face, he got a grip and swallowed back the rest of the anger churning inside him.

Damn it, this was one of the reasons he'd joined the military. No one in the navy cared who his family was. No one was impressed that he came from wealth. He'd joined the service right out of college, with one thought in mind: to get away from Boston and the never-ending feud between the Barones and the Contis. It had been going on for years and showed no sign of ending. If anything, the troubles between the families had picked up recently. What

with the fire and the disaster involving the new flavor gelato, the Barones were on red alert at all times
and looking for Contis under every rock.

Alex was tired of the potshots and anger. But he
was also a Barone and he owed the family his loy-
alty, even though he thought the adults on both sides
were idiots.

Now what he had to do was find a way out of
here, fast. He shot a quick glance around the restaurant. Curious stares pinned him in place, but his
friends were nowhere to be seen. They'd already
gone outside by the time Sal Conti had lost his mind.
Alex glanced at Daisy, saw her confusion and
wished he could explain all of this to her. But who'd
believe him?

In this day and age, who would expect two completely respectable, intelligent families to be so involved in a vendetta?

"You get out of my place," Sal told him hotly.

"Hey, I was just going."

"And you don't pay for your meal. We don't
need Barone money."

Disgusted, Alex said, "I'm not taking anything
from the Contis."

"Oh, for heaven's sake," Daisy muttered, stepping between the two men, only to be pushed gently
aside by Sal. You couldn't work at Antonio's without learning about Sal Conti's quick, volcanic temper. But Daisy was also well aware that the man

didn't have a violent bone in his body and that his temper disappeared as swiftly as it erupted.

But in this case she was pretty sure both men were nuts. Standing in the middle of a nice restaurant yelling at each other about ill fortune and curses was just crazy, no matter how you looked at it.

"You go sit down, Daisy," the older man said absently. "Get off your feet for a while."

She groaned, winced a bit and whispered, "I think it's too late for that."

A heartbeat or two passed before both men turned as one to look at her. At any other moment, she would have thought their twin expressions of sheer terror were funny. However, at the moment she had other things on her mind.

Daisy felt the contraction grab hold of the middle of her back and twist her spine into a pretzel. Every square inch of her suddenly erupted with a deep, throbbing pain that seemed to blossom and grow with every passing second. This was nothing like the annoying little twinges she'd been experiencing.

This was the kind of labor pain they wrote books about.

"I think I need to go home. Call the midwife," she whispered.

"Oh boy," Sal muttered, reaching for her left arm just as Alex grabbed her right. "You're okay, honey," her boss continued. Then he shouted, "Tony!"

Someone in the kitchen yelled back, "Yeah?"

"Call an ambulance. Call a hospital. Call somebody!"

Daisy managed a chuckle at the panic in Sal's voice, but when the contraction ended and was quickly chased by another, stronger one, that laughter faded into a low, deep moan of misery.

"I'll take her to the hospital," Alex said, and she shifted a glance at him. Navy pilot *and* a hero.

"No you won't," Sal countered, pulling Daisy closer to him. "We don't need help from a Barone."

"I'm not helping *you,*" Alex pointed out. He gave her arm a little tug, pulling her to his side. "I'm helping her."

"What is this," Daisy asked, yanking free of both of them, "a tug-of-war?"

"Hey, boss," Tony yelled from the kitchen. "Ambulance'll be here in fifteen minutes."

"Cancel it," Alex shouted, then looked down at Daisy. "I'll get you to the hospital. Let me help. Trust me."

She stared up into those chocolate-brown eyes of his and read determination there, along with an eagerness to help. And right then Daisy wanted all the help she could get. Besides, waiting fifteen minutes for an ambulance seemed like a lifetime.

"Okay," she whispered, dropping one hand to her belly. "Okay, good. Let's go."

"Daisy, I think—"

"It's all right, Sal." She looked at the older man who'd been so kind to her and forced a smile for his benefit. "I don't want to wait for the ambulance and— Ohhh…" She bent over, cradling her unborn child and biting her bottom lip to stifle the moan clogging her throat.

"That's it," Alex muttered, scooping her up into his arms. "We're outta here."

Waiters, customers and kitchen staff called out good wishes as Alex headed for the front door. The hostess rushed ahead and held the door open for him, reaching out to give Daisy's arm a pat as they passed.

Out on the street, Alex paused, Daisy in his arms, and looked to where the guys should have been waiting in their rental car.

Only one problem.

It wasn't there.

And neither were the guys.

"Oh, man…"

"What?" Daisy lifted her head from his shoulder.

"I think the guys took off."

"They left you behind?"

Alex grimaced and hitched her slight form a little higher in his arms. Amazing. Even pregnant, she was so slight, so fragile that she seemed to weigh almost nothing. But even as tiny as she was, it would be a long run to the closest hospital. Damn you, guys.

"Yeah," he said tightly, finally answering her question. "We do that sometimes. Go somewhere, then abandon one of the guys to make his own way back to the base."

"Why?"

He glanced at those blue-green eyes and lifted one shoulder in a shrug. "A joke. One I used to think was pretty funny."

"Swell."

Then she inhaled sharply and Alex felt her body tense. Terror rippled along his spine. He had to get her to help. Fast. "Cab. We need a cab."

And since he needed one, naturally there wasn't a single taxi to be seen. Ordinarily, a man could cross any Boston street by walking across the hoods of the cabs waiting in traffic. But not tonight. On this warm summer night, the air was still and so were the streets.

As horrible thoughts of running back into the restaurant to ask Sal for help raced through his brain, Alex realized exactly where they were. If he'd had a free hand, he'd have slapped himself in the forehead.

"No problem," he said, "we're good." He started walking at a long-legged, hurried pace.

"Where are you going?" Daisy demanded, already seeing the lights of Antonio's slip into the distance. The hospital was uptown and he was headed in the wrong direction.

"My sister's place," he muttered.

"Your sister?"

"Just a couple blocks away. She's a registered nurse. She'll know what to do."

"Are you kidding?" Daisy dug her fingers into his shoulder and talked through a pain that seemed strong enough to tear her in half. "*I* know what to do. Get to the hospital and deliver this baby."

"I know. I know. But there aren't any cabs—"

"The ambulance—"

"Look," he said as he kept moving, "we could go back to the restaurant and wait for the ambulance. Or we could go about a block and wait for an ambulance. My way, we'll have a registered nurse there to help. Which beats having a busboy or Sal deliver your baby."

"Okay, that makes sense."

He gave her a squeeze and moved even faster. "Trust me, okay? It'll be good. I'll take care of you."

"Why are you doing this? You don't even know me."

He looked at her. "Does it matter right now?"

She met those dark, deep eyes and heard herself say, "No. No, it doesn't matter."

As the next contraction rippled through her body, Daisy surrendered. She was in no position to hop out of his arms and race down the street, trying to find a cab on her own. Even if she'd wanted to. Which she didn't. For some reason, it felt good having him near. Being held as if she were something precious. Someone to be cherished. It had been so long....

No, that wasn't right. She'd *never* felt like this before. No one had ever cherished her. No one had ever truly cared. Not even the man she'd thought would love her forever. The man who'd given her a baby, then run off and gotten himself killed the moment he'd found out about the pregnancy.

She pushed thoughts of Jeff out of her mind. It wouldn't do any good to go back down that road. That time was over and done, and a whole new world was about to open up to her.

If she could just make it through labor.

Alex moved quickly. Streetlamps haloed the sidewalk with a soft, ivory light and a cool evening breeze slid in off the ocean, lightening the humidity like a gift from God. Up and down the street, people went about their business, completely ignoring the tall man with a pregnant woman in his arms. A group of kids skateboarded around them like a wave cresting around a buoy, but Daisy hardly noticed. She was much too involved with what was happening to her own body to care about anything else.

"Hang on, okay?" Alex whispered. "It's not far now."

"Boy, I hope not." Her fingers tightened on his shoulder again, then slowly, fractionally, relaxed. "I'm not an expert or anything, but I think this is it."

"Yeah, I got that."

"No, I mean *now*." Daisy felt as though everything inside her was struggling to push its way out of her body. And in the classes she'd taken, that was pretty much *D* hour. *D* as in delivery.

"Oh man, don't say that." He glanced down at her and held her more tightly to him. "Please don't say that."

"This isn't exactly how I'd planned to do this, you know."

"I know. But it's really close. I swear. Just hold on, okay?"

"The pains are coming so fast. Really strong, too." She tipped her head to look at him. In the glow of the streetlamp, his face seemed to pale a little, but Daisy told herself it was probably a trick of the lighting. At least, she hoped so. She didn't want to think that he was as scared as she was.

Heck, *somebody* should be in charge here.

"Don't push."

"What?"

"Breathe, breathe. Pant. You know." Then he demonstrated, and Daisy had to laugh despite the pain lancing through her middle.

"And where'd you learn that, fly boy?"

"Hey, I have a TV. I've seen movies." He grinned, but didn't look down at her. Instead, he kept his eyes fixed straight ahead, as if he could see his destination and wasn't about to be distracted from reaching his goal. "I know all of that stuff. Boil water. Pant. Don't push. Push."

"Well gee," she said, with a laugh that drifted

into a moan, "I feel much better now. I had no idea you were an expert."

"Yeah, well, I don't like to brag."

"An unusual man."

"Funny," he said, sparing her a quick glance as he rounded a corner and quickened his pace. "Just don't push anything out yet, whatever you do." He glanced both ways at the sporadic traffic, before sprinting across the street toward an old brownstone. "We're almost there. See? That's it."

Daisy held on to his broad shoulders and listened to the steady beat of his heart beneath her cheek. How strange. Two hours ago, she hadn't known this man existed. Now, on the biggest night of her life, he was all that stood between her and delivering her baby on the street, alone.

And though she should have been worried—after all, he was a complete stranger—she wasn't. There was almost a sense of peace in being held in his arms. As if it was where she belonged.

Okay, hysteria is probably not a good sign.

Where she belonged?

What was she thinking? Obviously, imminent birth put a strain on one's faculties.

He stopped in front of the well-kept old brownstone, and Daisy smiled in spite of the pain. She loved these old buildings. There was so much character, so much history in every single brick. It was one of her dreams to one day buy a run-down place and bring it back to life, help it to regain some of its past glory. Just as someone had done here.

In the glow of the porch light, Daisy looked at the dark red front door and the petunia-filled window boxes lining the front windows. A tiny garden, bursting with colorful blooms, filled the postage stamp-size plot between the brownstone and the sidewalk. The combined scents of summer flowers swept into the air, and Daisy inhaled them with her next deep breath.

Alex climbed the short steps, reached out and punched a buzzer, holding the button down with a steady, insistent pressure.

"If you don't let up on that button," Daisy reminded him tightly, "they can't answer, you know."

"Right. Right." He let it go and waited, tapping one foot on the concrete steps with a staccato rhythm that danced along his body and filtered into hers.

"Hey!" A disembodied voice floated out of the intercom. "Take it easy on the buzzer, huh?"

"Rita?" Alex's voice finally sounded strained, and Daisy couldn't help but be impressed that he'd managed to stay calm up until now. "It's me. Open the damn door, will you?"

"Alex?" The unseen woman's voice sharpened with concern. "What's wrong? Are you all right?"

"Do I sound all right?" He shook his head, muttered, "Sisters," then more loudly, he ordered, "Open the door, damn it."

A buzz sounded and the door snicked open. Alex pushed it wider with his foot. Stepping into the foyer, he kicked it shut behind him, then looked straight up.

Daisy matched his gaze, staring up the stairwell, following the line of the polished wood banisters that swept up and up the center of the four-story building. At the third floor, a woman's head suddenly appeared over the railing.

"Alex? What on earth is—" She broke off and gasped, so loudly that Daisy heard her sharp intake of breath.

"Rita," he called, "*help.*"

"Oh my goodness." She took in the scene in an instant and just as quickly began issuing orders. "Take the elevator, Alex. Go up to Gina's apartment. It's empty. I'll alert Maria and we'll meet you there."

"Right."

"Who's that?" Daisy asked, shifting her gaze to his face again.

"My sister the nurse. We'll call an ambulance and Rita can help till it gets here."

"Okay, good." Daisy glanced at the well-appointed reception area as he raced with her across the room. Overstuffed beige furniture was lined up against ivory walls. An ice-blue area rug lay in the center of the space, under a huge glass-and-oak table. Pale blue pillows were tossed here and there, giving the room a warm, inviting feel and the scent of fresh cut flowers filled the air. It was cozy, comfortable and peaceful.

But before she could notice much more, Alex was

at the old-fashioned elevator, pushing back the iron gate and stepping inside.

"How old is this thing?" she asked warily as he stabbed the fourth-floor button and the elevator lurched into motion.

"Don't worry. My dad made sure the elevator was brand-new and up to specs. He wouldn't trust his girls to some ancient elevator. He just liked the antique look."

"Glad to hear it." Truthfully, though, Daisy was just glad there was an elevator. With the pain now a constant companion, there was no way she would have been able to climb four flights of stairs.

When the elevator stopped and Alex threw the iron gate open, the first thing Daisy saw was his sister's sympathetic smile. "You poor thing. Don't you worry about anything, all right? You're safe."

Strange, Daisy thought. But she'd felt safe since the moment she'd first seen Alex back at Antonio's.

Three

Daisy barely had time to say hello before Alex's two sisters had swept her off and planted her in bed. Which was just as well, since she wasn't entirely sure she could speak without releasing the screams gathering at the back of her throat.

So she gritted her teeth and kept quiet as Alex left her in his sisters' care. In just a couple of minutes, the two women helped Daisy into a nightgown and tucked her into what was apparently yet a third sister's bed. The wide, brass bed creaked comfortably as she shifted higher onto the pillows and looked around the room. A large, cherry armoire stood against one wall and luxurious Turkish rugs dotted the shining wooden floors. It was a big, beautiful room. Nothing at all like her own small efficiency apartment.

"I don't feel right about this," she managed to say, and looked from one to the other of the women standing on either side of the bed.

The older of the two—Rita, that was her name—said, "Don't you worry, Daisy. This was our sister Gina's apartment, but she got married and moved out. For tonight, just consider it yours."

"I don't know…" But then the child within made another attempt at escape, and Daisy forgot all about feeling oddly out of place. Nothing was more important than the coming birth. Nothing.

"Do you want me to call anyone?"

Again Daisy looked at Rita. Her long, dark brown hair was pulled back into a ponytail and her chocolate-brown eyes were warm with concern. She smiled, and Daisy saw the resemblance between her and Alex.

"Sarah," Daisy said. "My midwife. Number's in my purse."

"Got it," the woman said. "Husband? Boyfriend?"

"No," Daisy said. "There's no one."

Rita shot her sister a quick look, then said, "Okay then, I'll call the midwife."

"Try not to worry, okay? I mean, just concentrate on your baby," the other sister, Maria, said, plump-

ing the pillow beneath Daisy's head as Rita hurried
out of the room. "I know this must be hard, but
honest to God, we're gonna take care of you. And
remember, Rita's a nurse."

"Thanks," Daisy muttered as the last of a contraction faded into the soft haze that signaled not the
end, but the beginnings of yet another, stronger pain
to come.

Maria, a shorter, younger version of her sister,
bustled around for a few more minutes. She tucked
and untucked blankets, smoothed sheets and patted
Daisy's hand in a distracted, nervous sort of way.
Finally, when she'd run out of things to straighten,
she announced, "I'm going to go make you some
tea," and left the room.

This just wasn't working out at all the way she'd
planned it, Daisy thought. And she'd spent plenty of
time planning for the birth of her child. She'd been
to a clinic for regular checkups and had even arranged for a midwife to come to her apartment to
deliver the baby. Sure, some of her friends had been
aghast at the idea of her delivering at home. But a
trained midwife was every bit as good as an obste-
trician—especially when the mother was young and
healthy, and no problems were expected. Sarah Lov-
ell was an excellent midwife, warm and caring and
far less expensive than an unnecessary hospital stay.
Which was an important consideration for a single
woman with limited health benefits.

Besides, Daisy had wanted to go through labor and delivery surrounded by familiar things. After all, she'd assumed that she'd be alone when giving birth, and at least in her own home, she'd feel safe…comfortable.

Instead, though, she was lying on a stranger's bed, with even more strangers hovering over her, asking if she was all right. *All right?* She was so far from all right she wasn't even in the same universe. Then Alex entered the room, pausing briefly in the open doorway. Her gaze met his and she felt a little bit better as she watched him cross the room in a few long strides. Funny how just a couple of hours ago she hadn't known he existed. Now his was the only familiar face in a world gone suddenly very weird.

"How you doin'?" he asked, leaning over her and brushing her hair back from her face.

"I've been better."

He smiled, and she thought, *That's easy for you to do.* Then the next pain hit and she bit down hard on her bottom lip to keep a screech from erupting.

He took her hand, enfolding it in his. Just having him hold on to her helped, and she drew on his strength when her own started to ebb.

"Squeeze my hand," she whispered through gritted teeth. The midwife had told her that during delivery she should try to keep her muscles as relaxed as possible, so she couldn't hold on to him.

"I don't want to hurt you," he said, but tightened his grip nonetheless.

"You won't. Tighter." His fingers clenched harder and it actually helped to distract her from the real spasms twisting her middle. Closing her eyes, she arched with the pain, trying not to fight it. Trying to remember that when this was all over, she would have her baby. She'd never be alone again. She would have someone to love. Someone who would love her back.

"Rita?" Alex turned to look at his sister as she hurried back into the bedroom.

"The midwife was out on another delivery. I left a message," she said, forcing a smile for Daisy before looking at her brother. "Alex, go away."

"What?"

"I want to check her progress. Leave."

"No," Daisy said, and could hardly believe she was saying it. But she simply didn't want to go through this alone. His warm strength reached down into the cold, dark corners inside her, and Daisy couldn't imagine letting go of that feeling. Not now. "Stay. Just don't let go of my hand."

Alex looked down into those pain-filled blue-green eyes and knew he wasn't going anywhere. She seemed so small, so alone. And yet she faced each pain as bravely as any military man he'd ever seen. She didn't back down. She didn't scream or complain. She simply braced herself and rolled with each progressively stronger contraction.

He looked down at her small hand as his fingers tightened around her fragile bones and a part of him wondered at the strength in her. Alone. No one to help her. No one to help raise this baby. She faced it all bravely—even though she was going through the biggest moment in her life surrounded by strangers.

"I'm not goin' anywhere, Rita."

Rita scowled at her brother, then smiled at Daisy. "It's okay. The midwife will get here eventually. But until she does, we'll do fine. I've helped to deliver lots of babies and even done a couple on my own in the ER. Mothers and babies are doing nicely."

Good to know. Very good, Daisy thought as another pain crested and she arched her back, riding it as though it were some invisible bucking bronco in a rodeo.

Her world became nothing more than the pain and Alex's grip on her hand. Nothing else mattered. Nothing else registered. Not Rita's tender hands or whispered words of encouragement. Nine long months had come down to this one moment in time.

Daisy's brain raced, trying to stay one step ahead of the pain, trying to remember that every contraction brought her one step closer to being a family. That any minute now she'd be holding her baby in her arms and the pain would be only a memory. Oh, she wished it was just a memory.

But that sense of peace hadn't hit her yet. What she needed at the moment was a distraction. Any distraction.

"Talk to me." She looked up at Alex and forced the words through gritted teeth.

He grabbed a nearby chair and drew it close to the bed. Sitting down, he kept a firm grip on her hand and said, "Sure. What should I talk about?"

"Anything. Everything." She sucked in a greedy gulp of air. "Just talk to me."

"Right." Alex shot a glance to the foot of the bed, where Rita was stacking clean towels and arranging a lamp for the best possible light. Maria was in the other room, probably pacing a trench in Gina's carpet. He shifted his gaze back to Daisy, smiled and started talking.

His words flowed over her, creating wonderful pictures that took her out of the lovely bedroom, away from the body-twisting agony of labor and into worlds and places she'd never seen before. She could almost see Alex at the commands of a navy jet. She nearly felt the G forces of takeoff and the meteoric rise as the jet climbed toward heaven. She sensed the freedom that flying gave him and she heard the joy in his voice as he described being a member of the navy's elite flight team, the Blue Angels.

He painted word pictures for her and she saw the incredible stunts he and his team performed miles above the earth. She could hear the oohs and aahs of the crowd as they stared, transfixed, at the intricately choreographed maneuvers the pilots made. And she sensed his regret that his time on the team was over. But the stories he told, the magic in his voice, were enough to take her mind off the torment in her own body, and for that, she'd always be grateful.

"I'll be reassigned when my leave's up," he continued, leaning in close to her, making her concentrate on his words rather than the pain. "Don't know yet where I'll end up, but—"

Daisy nearly flew off the bed. A sudden, desperate urge to push grabbed her and she clutched at Alex's forearm with a frantic grip. "Oh…oh God. Something…something's changed. It's different now. And…I think it's coming and—"

"Rita…"

Already in position, Rita lifted the edge of the thin blanket covering Daisy's legs, and when she straightened up again, she had a determined glint in her eyes. "Okay, honey. This *is* it. The baby's crowning."

"Oh, God." Finally. Her child. So close. Daisy's arms ached to hold it.

"Whatever it is," Rita added with a quick smile, "it's got a lot of hair."

Daisy's breath hitched and tears stung the backs of her eyes. Her baby. A tiny person. Almost ready to enter the world.

And she had to help.

"Have to push," she said. "Have to push now."

"You can't. Not yet. Just breathe, Daisy," Rita told her. "Let the baby ease down. It'll do most of the work now, if you just try to relax and let it."

"Relax?"

"I know," Rita said with a short laugh. "Easy for me to say. But you have to try. Pant. Short, sharp breaths. You can do it, Daisy."

"You can," Alex said, standing up to lean over her, drawing her gaze to his face. "You're plenty amazing, Daisy. You can do this."

She didn't want to. She wanted to push. She wanted the miracle over already. She wanted the pain to stop and her baby to be born. Oh God, she wanted to get up out of her body and run away.

Daisy twisted and writhed on the bed, planting her feet and rolling from side to side with the pain.

"Just a little longer, Daisy," Rita said. "You're doing great. Everything's terrific. Just a little longer. Be tough, okay?"

"Push," she whispered between pants as the driving, instinctive urge grabbed hold of her and demanded to be obeyed.

"Soon."

"Now."

"Look at me, Daisy." It was Alex's voice again, and she turned her head to look at him. Staring into his dark brown eyes, she concentrated on the way the light seemed to fill them, how warmth pooled in their centers and radiated toward her. "Concentrate on me, Daisy. You can do it. It's almost time. You've been great and now it's almost over. Just stay strong."

"Alex…" She said his name with an exhaled breath and it felt almost like a prayer.

Seconds ticked past into eternity and Daisy fought her body's instincts, trying to hold in the life fighting to get out. It made no sense, she thought wildly. It's time. "Have to—have to—"

"Okay, here it comes," Rita said, then added the most beautiful words Daisy had ever heard. "Push, Daisy. Push hard."

She did and felt her body tighten, grow stronger, as if a closely reined-in Thoroughbred had suddenly been turned loose and allowed to run. Pressure built to an unbelievable level until she heard Rita say, "Okay, now wait. The baby's turning. Pant, Daisy. Don't push. Hold on, hold on."

Alex stayed in her line of vision, forcing her to meet his gaze. She stared up at him and wondered how he'd come to be such an important part of her life in a few short hours. He was here. Sharing this moment with her. Making it his own as well as hers. And though she knew that it was only because they'd all been caught up in an emergency and that this sense of closeness wouldn't last, a part of her wished it could. Wished that somehow Alex and she were connected by more than a chance meeting at a restaurant.

"You're doing great," he said, and smiled in admiration. "Just hang on a few more minutes."

"I can't," she said, knowing it was true, feeling it down to her bones. She just couldn't do this for another minute. It was too hard. Too much. She wanted to stop now. She wanted to close her eyes and sleep. She wanted this to be *over.*

"Oh, yes you can." He leaned down closer until his face was just a kiss away from hers. "Daisy, I think you can do anything."

"One thing you can do," Rita said loudly from the foot of the bed, "is *push.* A couple more big ones will deliver your baby, Daisy."

"I'm tired...."

"I know." Rita glanced at her brother. "Sit behind her and prop her up. It'll help."

He took orders without question. A military thing, he guessed. Easing down onto the bed, he held Daisy against his chest and looked down, beyond the edge of the blankets just covering her modesty. And as he held her, he felt her body tense, felt her strength gather.

"Here it comes, Daisy," Rita called out, sounding

like the cheering section at Fenway Park. "Keep going, keep going."

Stunned, Alex watched in silent awe as a squirming, furious baby slipped from Daisy's body, took a deep breath and released an impressively loud screech of outrage. Laughing, Rita held the baby up for Daisy to see, and announced, "It's a girl and she's a beauty!"

"Oh, look at her," Daisy said, and collapsed against him.

Alex wrapped his arms around her and laughed along with his sister as the tiny, squalling piece of humanity let everyone know she thought the world was too bright and too loud and too cold. Rita worked quickly, taking care of the little things that had to be done, then wrapping the baby snugly in a soft towel. Laying the child in the crook of her mother's arm, Rita went about cleaning up the room while Daisy lay stunned, holding her family in the circle of her arms.

Four

——

Two hours later, the midwife had come and gone, and the room where Daisy lay with her daughter was quiet and shadow filled. The Barones had left her alone for a while, sensing, she thought, that she needed a little quiet time with her baby.

Daisy looked down at her daughter, cradled in her arms, and felt completely overwhelmed by the most powerful rush of love she'd ever experienced. She'd had no idea that the feeling would be so intense. So stunning in its ferocity. She felt as though she could do battle with a bear for this child and come out the winner. In an hour or two.

The baby screwed up her face and wiggled, and

Daisy thought it was all a miracle. The wonder of this child. The unbelievable kindness of the Barones, taking her into their home and treating her like royalty. Better. Like family. Something she'd never known—but recognized when she saw it.

Sarah, the midwife, had efficiently filled out the paperwork, given the new baby a thorough checkup and pronounced both mother and child in excellent health.

But Daisy could have told her that. She'd never felt better. Oh, exhaustion hovered at the edges of her mind, but all in all, she'd never felt more...*alive.* Adrenaline still pumped through her veins and she didn't think she could sleep even if she tried to close her eyes. Which she wasn't about to do. She was far too interested in staring at her little girl. She examined every finger and toe. Admired the sweet shape of her face and the curve of her tiny mouth. Mine, Daisy thought, and felt the flush of pride that she'd had a hand in producing this tiny, miraculous being.

In the soft glow of a dimly lit lamp, Daisy's gaze drifted over the sleeping baby. A soft brush of dark blond hair crowned her head. With her milky-blue eyes closed, her dark lashes spread like tiny fans on her cheeks, and her perfect rosebud mouth puckered and pouted as she dreamed of— What *did* babies dream of? Daisy wondered. Did memories of heaven flit through their minds? That would certainly explain why sleeping babies so often smiled. And it was a much nicer explanation than the gas theory most adults subscribed to.

Smoothing her fingertips across her baby's hands, Daisy marveled at the miracle of ten tiny fingernails. A soft breath puffed from her daughter's button nose and Daisy smiled. Such perfection. The baby screwed up her features, blew a spit bubble, then settled down again, and with every small movement, wormed her way further into her mother's heart.

How was it possible to love so deeply, so quickly? From the moment Daisy had laid eyes on her child, she'd known there was absolutely nothing on earth she wouldn't do for her. And the depth of that feeling was staggering.

"A dollar for your thoughts."

Daisy looked up as Maria stepped quietly into the room. Smiling, she asked, "A dollar? Didn't that used to be a penny?"

"Inflation." Maria grinned back and stopped beside the bed to carefully, tenderly, stroke one finger along the baby's soft cheek. She sighed wistfully. "So, *Mom*, how're you feeling?"

"Mom." Daisy repeated the word just to hear it again. It sounded…good. "I feel wonderful."

Maria shook her head and sat down on the chair beside the bed. "I don't know how you did it. When it's my turn—*if* it's ever my turn—I want a hospital bed, an operating room, a team of doctors and every single drug in the place."

Daisy laughed and winced as parts of her body ached in response. "That might have been nice," she admitted, but, glancing down at her baby, she said, "I wouldn't change a thing, though." Then she added a little guiltily, "Well, except for moving in on you guys. I'm really sorry about this. The baby and I will leave first thing in the morning, I swear."

Maria waved aside her apologies and leaned back in the chair. "Don't worry about it." Letting her gaze drift around the room, she said quietly, "Since Gina got married and moved out, we've really hated having this place empty. It's nice to be up here again." She paused. "There's no rush for you to move home. I mean, if you stay here for a few days, one of us would always be around to help out if you needed anything."

It worried Daisy just how much that idea appealed to her. Not that she didn't love her little apartment. She did. But the thought of having someone close by for her first few days of motherhood was a comforting one. After all, she'd read all the books, taken the nursing classes and talked to every mother she met at the restaurant. But actually being *in charge* of a helpless, new human being was just a little scary.

Having company might make the transition from single woman to mommy a little easier.

"Maybe I will," she said, telling herself that her desire to stay a bit longer had absolutely nothing at all to do with Alex. "Thank you for offering."

Maria grinned and shook her head. "No thanks necessary. Believe me, Rita would love to spend some extra time with the baby, and I'd enjoy the company, too. Like I said, it's nice to have somebody in Gina's apartment again. Feels wrong with it empty."

"It must have been nice," Daisy said, wondering what it must have been like to be a part of a huge, loving family. She guessed the Barones must be a close bunch, since the sisters shared this brownstone. "I mean, for all of you. Living here together, but with your own separate apartments."

"Oh, it's been fun...most of the time. But trust me, the separate apartments were a necessity." Maria grinned conspiratorially. She leaned forward, propping her elbows on her knees and her chin on her hands. "I love my sisters, but if we didn't have our own doors to close, well, let's just say we're all *very* Italian."

Instantly, Daisy flashed back to the scene at Antonio's and remembered how Sal and Alex had shouted at each other. Of course, anyone who worked with Sal would be used to his lightning-quick temper and his ability to shout over anyone except his aunt Lucia. The shouting didn't bother Daisy. Never had. Growing up in foster homes, you learned early to tune out arguments. Besides, there was something about a family that shouted at each other. As bizarre as it seemed, it at least meant they cared enough about each other to argue.

And everyone at Antonio's knew about the feud between the Conti family and the Barones.

She just hadn't realized that Alex was a member of the enemy camp until it was way too late to do anything about it. And honestly, she told herself, she didn't know if she'd have changed anything, anyway. She could still remember the feeling of being held in his arms, close against his chest. The feel of his hand on hers while she labored to deliver the baby; his soft, soothing voice as he talked and talked in an effort to help. No. She wouldn't have changed a thing. Alex Barone was...*nice*. And in Daisy's admittedly small experience, that was a rarity.

Her heart twisted just a bit as she allowed herself to wonder what her life might have been like if the father of her baby had been someone like Alex. She and her daughter would be loved. They would have a real home with family to care about and celebrate this child's birth. Instead, there was just Daisy and the baby. But that was okay, too, she reminded herself firmly. She and the baby would be fine. Just the two of them. And if she wished things could be different, if she should dream about a deep, rumbling voice and a pair of beautiful brown eyes, her daughter would never know about it.

"So, Alex said you work at Antonio's."

Daisy stopped thinking, which was probably just as well, considering where her thoughts had been moving.

"Yes," she said, grateful for something to think about besides Alex. "For a few years now."

Leaning back in the chair again, Maria lowered her gaze to the hem of her blouse and plucked at a loose thread. "Do you like it?"

"I do." Daisy smiled. "It's actually a lot of fun and I get to meet different people all the time. Plus the tips are pretty good."

"And the Contis…"

Daisy braced herself. She didn't want to offend any of the Barones. After all, they'd pretty much saved her neck tonight. They'd been kind and generous, and one of them had safely delivered her baby while another had held her hand and soothed her fears. So she spoke tentatively, wanting to be loyal to the people who employed her and treated her well, yet not wanting to offend the family that had helped her when she'd needed it most.

"Maria," she said, "I don't know much about this feud between your families, but I do know the Contis have always been very good to me and I—"

Instantly, Maria jumped to her feet and paced a few steps before whirling around to look at Daisy. "This stupid feud. It's ridiculous. It's the twenty-first century, for Pete's sake."

Surprised and relieved, Daisy asked, "So, you're not anti-Conti?"

Maria laughed, a short, harsh sound that seemed to scrape at the air. "I guess you could say that. For all the good it'll do me."

She looked so miserable all of a sudden that Daisy found herself wanting to help in some way. "If it makes you feel any better, not all of the Contis are interested in your family's war, either."

"Really?" Maria's dark gaze locked on her, and even from a distance Daisy could read the spark of hope there.

"Really," she assured the other woman. "Sal and his aunt Lucia are the angriest." And just thinking about the old woman who was the head of the Conti family was enough to give Daisy cold chills. Lucia was a cold-hearted woman whose perpetual anger at the world had drawn deep, ugly lines on her face and withered whatever spirit she'd once had. No. If Lucia had her way, every last Barone would be wiped from the face of the earth. But there was no point in saying that. "For whatever reason, Sal and Lucia have got a big grudge against the Barones. They never talk about it where any of us can hear it, but when the shouting starts, it's hard not to pick up pieces of information."

"I'll bet," Maria said glumly.

"That's just the two of them, though," Daisy

pointed out. "Bianca and Steven and their mother don't want anything to do with this feud."

"Really?"

"Oh yeah. Steven hates it when Sal goes on a tear about your family. He's even tried to defend the Barones once or twice. But Sal won't listen."

Maria released a breath and a slow smile curved her mouth. Swallowing hard, she said, "That's something, then, at least. Maybe things can change. Maybe it's not too late to— Oh!"

"Is something wrong?" Daisy asked as the other woman's face paled noticeably.

Maria swallowed hard again. "My stomach's a little…queasy. It's nothing." Clapping one hand to her stomach and the other to her mouth, she breathed slowly, deeply.

"Maria." Rita stuck her head in the doorway. "Geez. The woman just had a baby. Why don't you come on out and let her get some sleep?"

"It's okay—" Daisy began.

"Of course—" Maria said at the same time, making a visible effort to get control of her upset stomach. "Get some sleep, Daisy. I'll see you later."

As she left, Rita smiled. "Do you need anything?"

Need, no. *Want,* yes. Daisy wanted to see Alex. Wanted to know where he was and when—or if— he'd be coming back. Strange that she should feel such a connection to a man she hadn't known existed just a few short hours ago. But hadn't someone once said that battlefield friendships were the strongest because they were formed during trial and tribulation?

Well, what was labor but a battlefield?

Remembering Alex's warm, strong grip on her hand, the deep rumble of his voice and the calm reassurance in his eyes was enough to make Daisy's heart ache to see him again. They'd come through labor and delivery together, and that bond went deeper than she'd suspected.

But how could she say all of that to his sister? Why would Rita want an unwed mother to latch on to her brother? She wouldn't. So Daisy swallowed the questions she wanted to ask and instead said simply, "No, thanks. I don't need anything."

"Sure?"

"Yes, I'm sure. Besides, you've already done enough. I can't really even begin to thank you."

"Then don't try," Rita said, still smiling. "Being able to take part in your little miracle was something I'll always remember. I don't get to see many births in cardiac care."

Daisy's gaze dropped briefly to her still-sleeping baby. "She is a miracle, isn't she?"

"You're darn right. Now..." She pulled in a breath, blew it out and said in a rush, "I have to get downstairs. But Maria will be here until Alex gets back, in case you need anything."

Alex. The other woman saying his name made it seem all right to ask. "He left?" Daisy tried to make the question sound casual, but something in Rita's eyes told her she hadn't quite pulled it off.

"He'll be back soon."

"Oh," she said, "he doesn't have to—"

"Of course he does," Rita interrupted, glancing at the baby. "Even miracles need a change of diapers." She grinned. "He went out to pick up some supplies for the baby."

A deliciously warm feeling did battle with a pang of guilt. He hadn't run for the hills. He'd gone off to do her yet another favor.

"So why don't you take a nap while the baby's sleeping?"

"I think I will," Daisy said, and she was still smiling as Rita left.

Snuggling down deeper under the light blanket, Daisy cuddled her daughter close and planted a gentle kiss on her forehead. The lamp on the other side of the room glowed a pale yellow. Outside the window, dawn was just lightening the sky with pastel shades of rose and gold. Even through the double glass panes, Daisy heard the sounds of the city waking up and going about its business. But here, in this shadow-filled room, life was quiet, complete.

Her body ached, but her heart was full. The adrenaline pumping through her veins had slowed to a trickle, and fatigue pulled at her as she closed her eyes. She breathed deeply, slowly, letting herself relax, shutting off her busy brain until only thoughts of Alex remained. Then, closing her eyes, she willed herself to sleep, and planting the seeds for a lovely dream, her mind conjured up the image of Alex's smile.

By the time Alex rushed back to the apartment, carrying four bags of things no baby should be without, Rita had gone downstairs and Maria was asleep on the couch. He stashed the bags in the kitchen, woke his sister up and sent her off to her own apartment, then walked into Gina's former bedroom.

Pale, soft daylight crept through the window on the far side of the room and reached toward the woman sound asleep on the bed. Her long hair fanned out on the pillow beneath her head like a chestnut halo, framing her face with rich color. The dim morning light glimmered off the streaks of red and deep brown and highlighted a few strands of bronze that shone like old gold. Shadows lay beneath her closed eyes, but even in her sleep, she smiled and held her daughter close.

He watched the rise and fall of her breasts and reassured himself that she and the baby were fine. There was no reason to be worried. And yet a thread of concern wound through him, anyway. She was fine now. But what about later? What about when she went home, alone? Just she and the baby.

Alex scowled to himself at the thought. What the hell kind of man walked away from a woman like this? he wondered. What kind of subspecies of male turned his back on his own child?

And why did Alex care so damn much?

That thought stopped him cold.

Shoving his hands into his pockets, he leaned one shoulder against the doorjamb and crossed one foot over the other as he continued to study Daisy. Why did he care? What was it about this woman that had gotten to him in such a short amount of time? Was it the old knight-in-shining-armor-riding-to-the-rescue-of-a-lady-in-distress complex? Was he putting too much into this, making more of what he was feeling than was actually there?

No.

He couldn't buy that.

He'd never been the type to have a hero complex. He didn't go out of his way looking for people to save. This had just happened.

And now that it had, he wasn't at all sure what to do about it.

Pushing away from the doorjamb, he walked quietly into the room. Mother and baby slept on, blissfully unaware of his presence, which was just as well. He had a few things to think about and he knew that if Daisy opened her eyes and looked at him, his brain would refuse to work.

Taking a seat in the chair beside the bed, Alex

leaned toward them and reached out one hand. Gently, he smoothed Daisy's hair back from her face and smiled to himself when she sighed in her sleep and turned toward his touch. His fingertips slid tenderly across her cheek, and he marveled at the smooth silkiness of her skin and the tiny, near electrical surges of heat snaking straight up the length of his arm.

He'd never felt this instant and bone-deep reaction to any woman before. And he wondered what kind of man he was to have these feelings for a woman who'd just given birth.

But as he watched her sleep, Alex told himself that for now he wasn't going to question anything. He was just going to enjoy being here, standing guard in the shadows, with Daisy.

Five

***

The baby woke her.

In Daisy's dream, a kitten mewed softly, demanding attention. And when she opened her eyes, she realized it was no kitten, but her own daughter, wide awake and apparently hungry.

"She just woke up."

That deep voice was unmistakable. As were the goose bumps racing up the length of her spine. Shifting her gaze from her daughter's tiny, scrunched-up face to the man sitting in a chair beside the bed, Daisy felt her stomach flip-flop, and told herself she was an idiot.

Here she lay, a brand-new mother. A *single*

mother, thank you very much, mainly because she'd allowed her heart to rule her head. She'd mistaken a man's interest in her for love, and now she was...well, here. And she wasn't about to make the same mistake all over again. She couldn't afford to. It wasn't just her own happiness and well-being at stake now. There was her baby to think about.

Her daughter.

Her family.

Keeping that thought firmly in mind, Daisy met that deep brown gaze of his and resisted the urge to slide into the warm chocolate welcome she saw there. "I can't believe I almost slept through her waking up," she said, and turned her gaze briefly back to her daughter. A much safer plan. "What kind of mother does that make me?"

"A tired one," he said, leaning forward and bracing his elbows on his knees.

His dark gold shirt made his skin look even more tan, more bronzed. His shirt collar lay open, exposing a V of flesh that looked just as tanned as his face. His broad chest strained that shirt to the breaking point, and Daisy didn't even want to think about how long his legs looked in the worn denims he had on.

He smiled at her, and darn it, she noticed a flash of warmth in his eyes that jabbed at her, poking holes in her resolution to keep her distance. Oh, Alex Barone was one potent man.

"I think she'd have managed to get your attention in another minute or two."

Her mouth curved gently as she stroked the tip of one finger along her baby's cheek. "Isn't she amazing?"

"She's beautiful, all right," he said, his gaze locked on her until Daisy felt the strength of his stare and turned her head to look at him. "But I was just thinking that *you're* amazing, Daisy…" He paused, grinned and said, "I don't even know your last name."

"Cusak," she provided, adding, "There really wasn't a lot of time for introductions, was there?"

"Things were a little tense."

"Oh," she said with a laugh, "now there's an understatement."

Alex nodded, but didn't take his gaze off her. He couldn't seem to stop looking at her. And even while that thought registered, he wondered what in the hell he was supposed to do about it. This wasn't exactly a romance situation. God, the woman had just given birth, and he was sitting here thinking about— Well, it was probably better if he just steered his brain down a new path.

The baby mewed again and waved one tiny fist halfheartedly. Tearing his gaze from Daisy, Alex looked at the tiny scrap of humanity and found himself smiling again. So small. So helpless. A rush of something warm and tender filled him and Alex gave himself a minute to enjoy it.

"Do you have a name for her?"

"I've been thinking about that," Daisy said, and tried to shift into a more comfortable position on the bed.

Noticing what she was doing, Alex moved quickly. "Let me get her," he offered, and scooped up the baby expertly, nestling her in the crook of his left arm. Every Italian man was comfortable holding a baby. It was almost second nature. And apparently the infant sensed his confidence, because she settled down instantly, as though she'd only been waiting for him to hold her.

"Oh," he whispered, "you're a heartbreaker, aren't you?"

"She likes you," Daisy said, and he glanced at her. She'd pushed herself higher against the pillows. The deep rose nightgown she'd borrowed from Rita was a little big on her and the scoop neck opening dipped a bit too low for Alex's comfort. One of the straps slipped down off her shoulder, and between that and her tousled curls, she was an impossible combination of sexy innocence. She was enough to take his breath away. That soft smile on her lips wasn't helping anything, either.

Forcing himself to look away, he shifted his gaze to the baby and right away knew he was no safer. He looked down into those milky-blue eyes and felt

a hard, solid punch of something damn near inde-
scribable. It was as if the tiny girl was staring deep
inside him and reaching a part of him that had never
been touched before.

Caught by that sensation, Alex smoothed his fingertips over one of her tiny fists, and when she
grabbed hold of one finger and held on, he felt that
fragile grip all the way to his bones.

Alex sucked in a long deep breath and let it out
again slowly, thoroughly—an old trick he'd been
using for years when he needed to take a minute to
center himself. He hadn't expected to feel anything
for the baby. After all, he wasn't her father. But just
the same, he was caught up in the magic of her. In
the simple, beautiful miracle of her.

And it shook him.

Hell, he liked kids. Always had. He used to think
about someday having one or two of his own. But
that was before his fiancée broke their engagement
and swept aside all his thoughts of family.

Alex wiggled his hand, but the baby didn't release
her grip on his finger. Somehow he felt connected
to this newborn in a different way. He'd been a part
of her birth and a witness to the plain, simple miracle of her, and it had changed everything for him.

It's not just your mom who packs a wallop, is it?
he silently asked the infant.

Clearing his throat, he kept his gaze locked with

the little girl's as he asked her mother, "So what name did you come up with?"

Daisy's voice was soft and quiet and seemed as warm as the rays of morning sunshine that were just beginning to stream into the room. "Until tonight I'd been thinking of names like Sarah or Molly."

"Good names." He nodded, still looking into the baby's eyes, wondering what she would think of her new name. How it would affect her personality. How she would look as she grew into it over the years.

"But now..."

Daisy paused, and after a moment or two, when she didn't continue, Alex braced himself and shifted his gaze to her. She was staring right at him and the depths of her blue eyes rivaled those of her daughter's. The two of them made a formidable pair.

"Now?" he prompted.

"Now I think her name will be Angel."

Angel. "It suits her," he said, cuddling the featherlight weight close to his chest.

"And it will always remind me of tonight." A heartbeat passed. "Of you."

"Me?" It took a second for what she was saying to register, but then it hit him. The stories he'd told her while she labored to give birth. The memories he'd shared of his tour with the Blue Angels.

"I don't know what I would have done without

you tonight, Alex,'' she said, and the blue of her eyes darkened as she spoke, drawing him closer.

Holding the baby carefully, he moved to the edge of the bed, easing down gently so as not to jostle the child or the mother. ''If I hadn't been at the restaurant, Sal would have called an ambulance. You would have been all right, Daisy.''

''But I wouldn't have had you with me during the delivery. Your voice, your talking to me, helped get me through it.'' She reached out and laid one hand on his forearm, and Alex would have sworn he felt the heat of her touch right down to the soles of his feet. Damn, she packed a hell of a punch, even when she was obviously exhausted.

He couldn't wait to see what she'd be like once she got her strength back.

''Glad I could help,'' he said, his voice tight, thick with an emotion he hadn't expected. He was so damn touched he didn't really know what to say. Then he settled for the truth. ''I wouldn't have missed tonight for anything.''

The next couple of days passed quickly as Alex and Daisy eased into a routine of sorts that soon became all too comfortable.

She knew she shouldn't let herself start depending on his company, his help. But he was just so hard to resist. Those eyes of his were deep and dark enough to get lost in, and just hearing the sound of his voice kick-started her heart into a wild beat that nearly strangled her.

And it was all temporary.

She opened the window in Gina Barone's living room, stuck her head out and looked down at the street below. A soft ocean breeze drifted past, carrying the scents and sounds of the city. On the sidewalk, a couple of kids on in-line skates zipped past a flower stall, leaving the owner shouting curses as colorful as his carnations. The bakery on the corner was sending the tantalizing aroma of fresh bread into the air, and from somewhere in the distance came the sound of rock and roll blasting from a stereo.

Summer was just beginning to heat up, and soon the tourists would flood Boston. There would be some coming to see the monuments, some following the Freedom Trail and some just passing through on their way to somewhere else.

Like Alex.

Oh sure, his family was here, but he was a navy man. Which meant he never stayed anywhere for long. Daisy lifted one hand to the smooth, cool glass and drummed her fingers against it. She should leave now. Back away before it became even harder to distance herself from Alex Barone.

But then, she thought with a wry smile, that would be sort of like locking the barn door after the horse was already halfway down the road. She'd already become so accustomed to his laugh, his voice, the way he looked at her as if she was the most important person on the face of the earth.

She'd never known that feeling before and she was going to miss it.

Suddenly, the view seemed colder, lonelier, so she went back inside and carefully shut the window again.

Behind her, the front door of the apartment opened and closed, and even without turning, Daisy knew Alex had come in. She didn't need to hear the familiar sound of his footsteps on the gleaming hardwood floors. She sensed his presence in every single nerve ending.

Oh, she was in big trouble.

Swallowing hard, she turned to face him. He looked perfect, she thought. In his navy whites today, he was astonishingly handsome—like a poster boy for recruitment. Or one of the stars of that naval television show. But it was more than that. He looked as if he belonged in this casually elegant atmosphere. And he did—far more so than Daisy.

Quickly, she scanned the now familiar apartment, glancing from one exquisite treasure to the next— from the silk sofas to the Chinese vase to the other assorted antiques. And even as she appreciated the beauty of the place, Daisy felt like an onion in a tulip patch.

Alex and his family took these things for granted. Heck, he could probably tell her the specifics on most of the pieces in the room. And that thought only served to underline how very little she and the gorgeous navy pilot had in common.

His eyes locked on her from across the room, and she felt the power of his gaze even at a distance.

"You hungry?" he asked. "I bought Chinese after my meeting."

"Sure," she said, and swallowed hard. This was ridiculous. Nothing in common? Why should she care? There was nothing between them and there wasn't going to be. He'd been nice. Nothing more. And the chances of that changing anytime soon were slim to none. She was a single mom and he was just…single. Not to mention the fact that they came from two wildly different worlds. Why on earth would he be interested in her?

Answer: He wouldn't.

And boy was that depressing.

"That didn't sound real convincing."

"Sorry." Daisy forced a smile. No point in giving him any clue as to what weird thoughts were racing through her mind. It had to be some kind of postpartum thing. Didn't all women go a little whacko right after giving birth? Sure. That was it. As soon as she was in her own place and back to her everyday life, she'd be fine. Of course, she wouldn't be seeing Alex anymore. But that was probably for the best, anyway.

"Come on," he said, and led the way to the

kitchen. "I swear, you're gonna love this stuff. I got it at Chang's, the best Chinese restaurant in Boston."

All right, Daisy, get ahold of yourself here. Be friendly and not sappy. "It smells wonderful."

"Tastes even better." He plopped the bag onto the butcher block island. "When I came in, you looked like you were doing some pretty serious thinking."

She flushed, darn it. She actually felt heat fill her cheeks. "Not really," she lied. "Guess my mind was just wandering."

"Anywhere in particular?"

Oh yes. But she couldn't exactly tell him that, could she? She stalled and looked around the pretty, efficient kitchen. With white walls and white appliances, the room practically glowed. If it had been Daisy's, she would have painted the cabinets a nice lemon yellow, but she absolutely loved the hand-painted porcelain sink. The herbs in the garden window over the sink looked bedraggled and neglected. They were as out of place in the neatly kept kitchen as Daisy was in the apartment itself. Suddenly she felt a lot of sympathy for the poor, forgotten herb garden.

"Just…" Her brain scrambled as she searched for something—anything—to say. She watched him unload several white cartons.

"Just what?"

"I was thinking that I should probably be going home soon."

He stopped short, his hand in the silverware drawer, his gaze on her. "Already? It's a little soon. I mean, you just had a baby and— There's no rush, you know. You can stay as long as you like."

"I know." And that was the problem. The longer she stayed, the longer she *wanted* to stay. Which would only make her eventual leaving that much harder. "Rita and Maria have both told me that over and over." They'd been wonderful. But Daisy couldn't help wondering if Alex's sisters would be feeling so generous if they knew that she was developing a thing for their brother.

"So, then, what's the big hurry?"

She pulled out a chair and eased onto it, her body still a little tender for quick movements. Propping her elbows on the tabletop, she looked up at him. "It's not like I'm racing out of here, Alex. But I don't belong here. And I have a home."

He snatched up a couple of forks, ripped two paper towels off the roll on the counter, then took a seat opposite her. Handing her a plate, fork and napkin, he started opening the small cartons and instantly, the delicious scents of beef and broccoli, cashew chicken and shrimp fried rice filled the room.

"Yeah, I know you do," he said, helping himself

after she'd taken a serving of rice. "It's just that I thought you were sort of enjoying it here and I—"

"Oh, Alex, it's been great. You've been great. And your sisters, too. But—"

He set his fork down with a clatter and leaned back in his chair, folding his arms across his chest. That uniform of his fit him like a second skin and made his tanned flesh look even darker. Rows of ribbons decorated his left breast pocket and Daisy wondered what he'd done, what dangers he'd had to face to win those medals.

"Look, Daisy," he said, "I know what it's like to want to be in your own place." He laughed shortly, sitting up to brace his arms on the table. "Hell, coming from my family, the first thing I can remember wanting was my own place."

She shook her head, not believing him. "Your family's terrific, Alex. And I've seen you with your sisters. You're very close." A part of her that had been lonely for years really envied him the closeness he shared with his family.

"Oh, they are," he agreed. "There's just too many of 'em. So I do understand that you want to be back on your own turf."

"Thank you."

"But," he added with a lopsided smile that seemed to hit her even harder than a full on blast might have, "why be alone right now if you don't have to be?"

God, it was tempting. So tempting. But she couldn't afford to allow herself to count on him. "Alex, you're on leave. If I stay here, you'll just feel like you have to keep me company, and I know you've got other things you have to do."

"Wrong." He pushed the carton of chicken toward her. "Leave means I get to do whatever the hell I want to do." He opened a carton of egg rolls and offered her one. "And what I want to do is spend time with you and the peanut."

A twist of something that was probably longing rippled through Daisy when he used the nickname he'd bestowed on Angel. Stalling, she took an egg roll and bit into it, savoring the tangy spices.

"So, what do you think?" he asked. "You'll stay a while longer?"

She shouldn't.

If she had any sense at all, she'd pack up Angel and their few belongings and grab a cab back to her apartment.

That was the smart thing to do.

The safe thing.

But Daisy had been trying to do the smart thing most of her life, and look where it had gotten her.

So for once in her life, she did what she shouldn't. She went with her heart.

"A few more days," she said, and when Alex grinned at her, Daisy's heart turned over in a painful twist she told herself she'd better get used to.

Six

By the end of the week, though, Daisy couldn't put off leaving any longer. She needed to get back to the real world. *Her* real world, anyway. As hard as it would be to leave the comfort and warmth of the old brownstone, she had to do so.

Rita and Maria were wonderful about it. Though the three of them had become fast friends, Alex's sisters understood her need to get back to her own place. To start seriously nesting, just she and the baby.

Alex, on the other hand, didn't seem to get it.

"I don't understand," he said for what had to be the fourth time in the last half hour. "Why are you in such a big hurry to leave?"

"I've been here a week, Alex," Daisy reminded him as she lay the baby on the bed so she could change her diaper.

"And...?" He sat down on the mattress near Angel, then stretched out alongside her, one hand smoothing her soft blond curls.

"*And*," Daisy countered, "I have a life. And an apartment—though not on the scale of this one— and it's time to get back to it." There. She'd pretty much been rehearsing that little speech all night. And it sounded so convincing even she nearly believed it.

"You can't have a life here?"

She shot him a look and felt the zing of something wild and rich and hot whip through her bloodstream. Which was another excellent reason for leaving. Honestly, did his eyes actually get darker when he wanted to get his own way? Had he perfected the art of looking both extremely masculine and cuddly at the same time?

Daisy affixed the tapes of her daughter's diaper, then snapped up the legs of the little pink sleeper that had been a gift from Maria. "Yes, I could have a life here," Daisy said softly. "It just wouldn't be mine."

"Okay," he said after a long, thoughtful pause. "You win."

"Gee, thanks."

"Hey," he said, "you should probably write this

down in a journal or something. My family can tell you how rare it is for me to say those words."

"I appreciate it."

"I don't like to lose."

"You haven't lost anything," she reminded him as he sat up and, as if it was second nature to him now, scooped her daughter into his arms and nestled her close to his chest.

Lifting his gaze to hers, Alex said quietly, "Yeah. I have."

Something like a swarm of bees took flight in the pit of her stomach, and Daisy told herself not to make more of that statement. He was just being nice and didn't mean at all what her out-of-alignment hormones were hoping he did.

"Alex—"

"So," he interrupted as he stood up, still holding the baby as if she were a part of him. "You're all packed?"

Daisy gave him a wry smile. "It didn't take long. I didn't arrive with much, remember?"

Reaching out, he smoothed her hair back from her face, then let his fingertips glide down the line of her cheek and sweep under her chin. Tilting her gaze up to his, he looked at her steadily for a long minute, then said, "Always."

When he and the baby left the room, Daisy plopped onto the mattress. When a woman's knees turned to water, she reasoned, it was sit down or fall down.

Her apartment building was nothing special. Clean and impersonal, the depressing beige walls of the lobby were decorated only by a line of mailboxes. Daisy stopped off at hers, and Alex was surprised to see how little mail had built up in a week. A couple of bills, an ad circular or two and that was it. Nothing personal. Nothing showing that someone, somewhere, had missed her.

Having grown up in a family large enough to field its own baseball team, he had a hard time imagining being so completely alone. And he didn't like to think of Daisy being lonely.

Damn it.

As they stepped into the waiting elevator, Alex carried the small suitcase Rita had provided to transport the things Daisy and the baby had accumulated in the last week. He listened to the hum and hiccup of the elevator and frowned as he rested one hand on Daisy's shoulder in an instinctively protective gesture. The damn thing sounded like it was on its last legs.

He made a mental note to look into it with the building super before he left.

The elevator paused at the third floor, the doors slid open agonizingly slowly and a long-haired guy with ripped jeans and a dirty T-shirt got on. He gave

Daisy a long, leering look that had Alex wanting to pummel him. But Daisy paid no attention. As wrapped up as she was in her baby daughter, she probably wouldn't have noticed if a streaker had walked onto the elevator.

Which worried Alex even more.

Hell, if she paid no attention to her surroundings, how in the hell would she be safe? And if she wasn't at his sisters' place, how could he *keep* her safe? The fact that that really wasn't his job didn't seem to register with him.

On the fourth floor, the guy in the torn jeans got off and gave Daisy a last leer as he loped down the hallway.

"Who was that?" Alex asked.

"Huh? What?" She lifted her gaze to his.

"That guy. The one practically drooling on you. Who was he?"

"Oh. I don't know," she said as the elevator doors closed and they started up again. "I don't really know many people in the building. Did he look nice?"

"Did I mention the drool?"

She laughed, and despite the flicker of anger sputtering through him, a part of Alex responded to the sweet, nearly musical sound. "Right," she said. "Drooling over a woman who just gave birth. Because I'm just so irresistible."

Damn straight.

But she simply didn't see her appeal. Those wide blue-green eyes, soft chestnut hair and the fragility that belied her strength did something to a man. Made him want to go find dragons to slay for her. Made him want to do stupid things like throw his coat over a puddle, like good ol' Sir Walter Raleigh, who'd given every other male in history a bad name.

Daisy touched something in him Alex hadn't thought about in years. Not since his fiancée had broken their engagement on Valentine's Day two years ago. Back then, he'd thought he'd had it all. A gorgeous woman to love, a fascinating career and a future with no boundaries except the ones he would set himself.

Then the Barone curse had reared its ugly head.

Well, at least his parents blamed his broken engagement on the curse. Alex had just been blindsided by a woman who'd gone from red-hot to icy cold in sixty seconds flat. Hell, he still wasn't sure why Megan had taken off, though he didn't miss her anymore. When he'd recovered from the hurt and his heart was mended, he'd vowed to steer clear of the ''permanent'' kind of woman. He wasn't about to risk being thrashed again.

Not that he'd become a monk or anything. He had plenty of women. More than his fair share, probably. But they were women who were no more interested in happily ever after than he was. They shared some laughs, some sex and then said goodbye, no hard feelings.

Until Daisy Cusak appeared and knocked every logical thought clean out of his head.

Now he was getting in way too deep with a woman who was so much the permanent kind she practically had an imaginary white picket fence surrounding her.

The elevator stopped at the fifth floor, and the doors opened onto a long hall that was just like every other hall in the building. Same beige paint. Same iron-gray industrial carpeting. Same stainless steel light sconces on the wall every five feet. Same sad, narrow window at the end of the hall.

Sunlight streamed in through the bare window, adding brightness to what would otherwise be a dismal scene. But again Daisy paid no heed to anything but the baby in her arms. She took off down the corridor, with Alex just behind her. Each door they passed looked exactly like its neighbor.

Beige.

God, he could really learn to hate that color.

She stopped at the fourth door on the left, and when he came up behind her, Alex had to smile. Naturally, Daisy's door would be the one distinctive note in an otherwise grim place.

Her door had been painted a bright, glossy sunshine yellow. Affixed to the door was a brass knocker in the shape of a sleeping cat, and engraved on its tail in a flowery script was the name Cusak. In front of the door lay an old-fashioned welcome mat.

"I like your door," he said simply, though in truth he meant so much more. He liked her attitude. A single mother, she wasn't worried about being alone, just wanted to get on with her life. Living in a world of beige, she'd refused to be beaten down by it and instead had chosen to fight back with a splash of defiant color. He admired people who stood up to the world and fought for a piece of it on their own terms.

Daisy smiled at him as she dug in her purse one-handed for the key. "I like bright colors," she said simply, then grinned as she came up with the key like a diver bringing up a piece of prized salvage.

She unlocked the door, threw it open and stepped inside, Alex right behind her.

Instantly, Daisy felt a wild mixture of pleasure and trepidation. She hadn't known until this moment just how much she'd missed her own little apartment. Everything familiar reached out welcoming arms to her, and she smiled to be back in a place that was so much a part of her.

But she was also a little hesitant about having Alex here. Her home was so very different from what he was probably used to. And it bothered her to realize just how much she wanted him to like it. She'd poured so much of herself into decorating the

tiny apartment that if he felt uncomfortable here—
or worse, just plain hated it—it would be as if he
was rejecting her, too.

She needn't have worried.

"This is great," he murmured as he walked past
her into the room.

Her gaze followed his, noting everything that he
was seeing for the first time. A veritable rain forest
of slightly droopy water-starved plants covered
nearly every flat surface. Potted daisies and African
violets vied for space with ferns and various colored
coleus. English ivy trailed from three different pots
and had been trained to stretch out leafy arms to
embrace framed photographs of faraway cities.
Paris. Madrid. Moscow. Athens. Dublin. All of the
places Daisy hoped to visit one day.

As Alex did a slow turn to look at everything,
Daisy noted the colorful rag rugs dotting the worn
gray carpet. She saw the overstuffed furniture and
tried not to compare it with the lovely silk pieces
she'd left behind at Gina's place. The Barone apartments were beautiful, but this was home—the nest
she'd made for herself and her child—and she was
proud of what she'd accomplished here. The warm,
soft afghans she'd crocheted herself, the pillows
she'd sewn and stuffed, the pale yellow paint she'd
applied to the kitchen cabinets…everything here
was *hers*. And for a girl who'd grown up with nothing to call her own, that meant everything.

But it surprised her to realize that she cared what Alex thought of her home. She half held her breath and waited for his reaction. When it came, she wasn't disappointed.

He looked at her and smiled, with warm approval shining in his eyes. "I like it. It's...cozy."

"Thank you." Pride filled her and she was suddenly ridiculously glad to have him here. "I'll just go put Angel down in her crib."

Daisy walked past him, through the small living room, to a tiny hallway leading to the bathroom, her bedroom and the nursery. Angel's room was the smallest, but here, too, Daisy had left her stamp of originality.

The walls were painted a soft sky blue, and clouds had been sponged on in a pale shade of cream. The effect was like a summer day and showcased the sections of picket fencing she'd nailed to the wall and the flowers she'd painted coming out from behind the slats. The crib was secondhand, given to her by one of the waitresses. But Daisy had painted it white, then made the sheets and comforter and bumper pads in a boldly striped fabric of blues and greens and yellows. A whitewashed rocker sat in one corner and a narrow chest of drawers stood against the far wall. Beside the crib was a small square table boasting a lamp with a Little Bo Peep lampshade.

"You did all of this, didn't you?"

He'd followed her in, and somehow hearing his voice in her house seemed…right. Which should have worried her. But she was just too darn happy to be home to care about that at the moment.

Laying her sleeping daughter in the crib, Daisy turned around to look at him. "Yes, I did. I like painting and fixing things up."

"You're good at it."

"Thanks."

He leaned one shoulder against the doorjamb and shoved his hands into his jeans pockets. He looked so darn good standing there that Daisy had to remind herself not to get attached. But she was pretty sure it was too late for those kinds of warnings.

"Makes me wonder what you could do with the BOQ on base."

"BOQ?"

"Bachelor officers quarters. They're about as sterile as you can get."

"You can do wonders with a little paint."

"Some of us apparently can," he admitted. His gaze dropped, drifting over her from her head to her toes and then slowly back up again. She felt it as surely as she would have if he'd touched her.

Her skin was humming and her breathing quickened in response to a flash in his eyes. And suddenly Angel's room was too small. Too enclosed. But then, the way she felt around Alex, Daisy had a feeling that Fenway Park would seem too intimate.

"Thank you for bringing me home," she said, and swallowed hard. Bracing herself, she slipped past him and out of the room, somehow managing not to shiver when her arm brushed against his chest.

"No problem."

He followed her into the living room, and when she simply stood there, obviously waiting for him to go, Alex took the hint. He headed for the front door, oddly reluctant to leave. Oh, he knew he should. But then, when did he ever enjoy doing what he was supposed to do?

"Look," he said, stopping so sharply that she ran into him from behind. He turned quickly, grabbed her shoulders to steady her, and tried to ignore the heat rushing from his hands into her and back again. Damn, there was some kind of powerful connection here. "How about I go get dinner?"

"Alex, you don't have to do that."

"I know I don't have to. I want to."

"I don't know…."

"You have to eat, right?"

"Yes."

"Well, so do I." His fingers tightened on her shoulders. "And I hate eating alone."

She smiled and shook her head. "You don't have to eat alone. You have a big family and probably lots of friends who've been wondering where you've been for the last week."

He grinned back at her. "You're prettier than any

of them. And frankly, I'd rather look at you over the table.''

She thought about it. He could almost see the wheels turning in her mind, and he wanted to tell her to stop thinking. To just feel. He knew damn well that she was experiencing the same sensations he was when they were together. Wasn't that worth exploring a little further?

What did they have to lose?

''Come on,'' he prompted. ''What'dya say?''

She started to shake her head, so he cut her off at the pass. ''I'll make you an offer too good to refuse.''

Daisy laughed. ''You sound like a gangster movie now.''

''No machine guns, I promise. Just the best pasta you've ever had.''

''Hmm. From which restaurant?''

He gasped dramatically and slapped one hand to his heart. ''You're kidding, right? You think an Italian would go out to *buy* pasta?''

''No?''

''Boy, have you got a lot to learn.''

''I guess so,'' she said, still chuckling.

Her laughter ended, though, when he leaned in and planted a quick, soft kiss at the end of her nose. ''And, honey, I'm just the man to teach you.''

Seven

The kitchen smelled wonderful.

Daisy sat at the small table for two tucked into a corner of the narrow room, and watched Alex as he cooked. He'd come back from the grocery store laden down with bags. Not only had he brought supplies for the dinner he wanted to cook, but he'd picked up a few basics for her as well. Thoughtful, Daisy told herself. Gorgeous, rich, thoughtful, navy pilot, sexy, tender.

Good heavens.

He was like the hero in a romance novel.

And way out of her league.

But that was okay, she reminded herself sternly,

because she wasn't looking for a man. She had enough to deal with right now. She had a new baby. A future to plan. She wasn't looking for romance. Actually, she was in no position to be looking for romance even if she'd been interested. Which she wasn't.

Not so very long ago, Daisy had thought love was the answer to everything. She'd trusted Jeff when he'd told her he loved her, believed him when he said she was all he wanted. She'd told herself he was just too nervous to ask her to marry him. And God help her, she'd been so sure he would be as happy as she'd been when she found out she was pregnant.

It hadn't taken long for the truth to surface.

She could still see the look in his eyes when she'd told him. If she allowed herself, she'd be able to hear him, too. *"Are you nuts? A baby? I didn't sign on for a baby. No way are you trapping me into this."* Then he'd hopped into his convertible and taken off with a squeal of tires so loud it had sounded like screaming.

Two hours later, he was dead. Killed when a truck ran a red light and plowed into the flashy car he'd thought so much of.

Daisy pulled in a deep breath and pushed the memory of Jeff into a dark corner of her heart. The love she'd had for him had died out as she'd watched him drive away from her in a near panic.

But she would always be grateful to him for giving her Angel.

"The secret," Alex was saying, "is the sweet sausage. Some people like regular pork sausage, but to get the rich flavor, you need Italian sweet sausage."

"I'll try to remember that."

He glanced at her from the stove and must have read the emotion in her eyes. "Something wrong?"

"No. Just thinking."

"Not exactly happy thoughts, then, I'm guessing."

"Navy pilot *and* a mind reader, huh?" She smiled to take the sting out of her words.

"I don't have to be a mind reader, Daisy. I can see storm clouds in those pretty eyes of yours."

She shifted uncomfortably in her chair. It had been so long since she'd received a compliment of any kind, she wasn't actually sure how to respond. Thankfully, he didn't wait for one.

"So," he said, reaching for the bottle of red wine he'd been letting breathe for twenty minutes. He filled her glass with water, his with wine, and carrying them, went back to his post beside the sauce pot and lifted his own glass for a sip. "Tell me about you."

"There's not much to tell." She took a sip of water.

"Then it shouldn't take long," he quipped.

A smile twisted the corners of her mouth. "Okay," she said, leaning back in her chair, clutching the wineglass with both hands. She stared down into the clear water and said, "I grew up in California."

"You're a long way from home."

"No," she said softly, "this is home now." In fact, she hadn't had a home until she'd come here several years ago. "You come from a big family, right?"

"Oh, yeah." He took a drink of wine and waited, his gaze on hers.

"I didn't. My folks died when I was five, and I grew up in the foster care system." There it was, she thought. That split second flash of pity that she usually saw in people's eyes when they found out the truth about her. It irritated her to see it in Alex's eyes, though. She didn't want to be pitied. It made her feel like that little girl in a hand-me-down dress again. And she certainly didn't want to go back there.

"That must have been rough."

"Don't feel sorry for me," she said, stiffening her spine automatically. She'd put a stop to pity parties when she was twelve, and she wasn't about to hold one at this late date.

"I don't."

"Huh?" She looked at him, curious.

"I don't feel sorry for you," he said, and leaned one hip against the chipped Formica countertop.

"Well, that's new." And it totally belied the emotion she knew she'd seen in his eyes.

"Why would I feel sorry for you? You've got a nice place here, a good job and a gorgeous new daughter."

Pride filled her. She'd worked hard to build a life for herself and she was glad he'd noticed. But she'd seen the pity flash, even though it had disappeared an instant later.

"But that said," he pointed out, "I'd be a real bastard if I didn't feel some sympathy for the kid you once were. Geez, Daisy, no child should have to grow up without a family."

She'd always felt that way, too, but hearing him say it aloud brought a twist of guilt. Angel would be growing up without a family, in the traditional sense. But as soon as that thought occurred to her, Daisy dismissed it. This was different. Angel would be loved and she would never doubt it. Angel would have her mother. Always. And that would be enough.

Daisy would make it be enough.

"That was a long time ago," she said, refusing to stroll down that particular memory lane. She'd come out of the shadows years ago and she quite liked the sunshine.

"I know," he said. "But it still feels like yesterday sometimes, doesn't it?"

"If I let it," she admitted, then straightened up and took a long drink of wine. "But I don't."

Alex nodded as he watched her. He'd seen the vulnerability on her face before she'd wiped it away with a practiced smile and a glint of determination. He had a feeling her past wasn't as far in the background as she'd like him to think. But there was nothing he could do for the child she'd once been. Besides, he told himself, she'd grown past it. Survived. Triumphed. She didn't need him to go back in time and rescue her, as much as he liked the idea.

"Anyway," she said, continuing quickly, obviously eager to get past the whole "poor little orphan" thing. "When I was old enough, I left. Got my high school diploma and went to the opposite side of the country for a fresh start."

He stirred the sauce and inhaled the familiar scent that made him think of big Sunday dinners with the family. "Boston must have been a huge change for you. How'd you like your first winter here?"

She laughed, and he watched her eyes light up. "Oh boy, that was a real shocker. I'd never even *seen* snow until I moved here."

"I always loved it when I was a kid," he said, remembering the countless battles he and his brothers and sisters had waged. The snow forts, the stockpiled pyramids of snowball ammunition, his sisters' sneak attacks. He smiled just thinking about it and felt bad all over again that Daisy had no such memories.

"Sure, when you're a kid, you're just worrying about playing in the stuff. But grown-ups have to de-ice windshields and spread kitty litter on the sidewalks and…" She stopped, smiling. "But you know all that. You grew up with it. For me, it was a real eye-opener, I can tell you."

"I'll bet."

"I love it, though." She shifted her gaze to stare out the tiny window as if she were watching a blizzard blow in. "It's so beautiful. And peaceful. And quiet, somehow. It's like the world takes a deep breath and holds it."

He watched her and thought that if the world stopped right now, he could spend eternity just looking at her. The play of sunlight on her features, the way her blond hair seemed to nearly glow, how her lips parted in a soft smile that was at once seductive and so innocent… Daisy Cusak was getting to him. Deep down inside. And he wasn't entirely sure he wanted to stop it from happening.

Which should have worried him.

The fact that it didn't worried him even more.

The next couple of weeks flew by.

Her maternity leave from the restaurant was going

by so fast, Daisy could hardly believe it. And that was mostly due to Alex.

He spent nearly every day with her and Angel. When she knew he was on his way, Daisy caught herself watching the street below for a sign of him, like a teenager waiting for her prom date to show up. She knew it was a mistake. Every night she lay awake in her bed and told herself that she should put a stop to it before things got out of hand. And every morning she leaped for the phone when it rang, hoping it was him.

It was nuts and Daisy knew it. Though she really enjoyed spending time with him, there was always a logical little voice in the back of her mind reminding her that this wasn't real. Sooner or later, Alex would be shipping out. As a naval pilot, he'd be going wherever they sent him, and she'd be nothing more than a quickly fading, pleasant memory. But then, even if he wasn't in the navy, even if he was staying here, in Boston, this situation wouldn't continue for long. Daisy was a nobody—and one of these days, Alex Barone would realize that. He came from a wealthy, influential family. She came from… Heck, she didn't even know what she came from.

And she was suddenly very glad that Angel was as tiny as she was. At least the baby wouldn't have any real memories of the man who'd invaded their world for a short time. Angel wouldn't miss him.

Wouldn't wonder where he was, if he was safe, if he was thinking about her.

Though her brain raced with the inevitable good-bye to come, Daisy told herself to relax, stop thinking and just enjoy Alex while he was there. After all, having a gorgeous, kind, thoughtful man pay attention to you wasn't all bad.

"So what do you think?" Alex asked. The tone of his voice told her it wasn't the first time he'd posed the question.

"Hmm?" She came up out of her mental wanderings and blinked.

"The picture?" he prodded, smiling. When she still didn't respond, he nodded toward the storefront window on the street beside them.

The words *Kid's Pix* shimmered in neon-green and yellow above the open doorway to the shop. In the display window was a darling portrait of a laughing baby dressed in a tiny tiger suit.

Daisy smiled and shook her head. "Angel's too young to be much of a photography subject. She'd sleep right through it."

He glanced down at the snoozing baby, comfy in her stroller. "Probably," he conceded, then lifted his gaze to Daisy's. Her stomach did the odd pitch and roll she was getting all too familiar with around him. "But it doesn't matter. You'll be holding her, anyway."

"Me?" She looked from him to the photography

shop and back again, shaking her head all the while. "I don't think so. I mean, I'm not dressed for having my picture taken and—"

"First, you look beautiful," he said, "and second, don't you want a nice picture of you and the baby? Something you can show her when she's a teenager and you want to remind her that you knew her when?"

Daisy's lips twitched. "I suppose your mother did that?"

"Oh yeah." He shifted his feet into a wide-apart, braced-for-anything stance and folded his arms across his chest. Something he usually did when he was about to get stubborn, Daisy'd noticed. "Mom had stacks of incriminating photos of all of us. One wrong move and she was liable to show naked bath pictures to our friends."

"She was not."

Alex tilted his head to one side and looked thoughtful. "You know, she never actually *did* it, now that you mention it. At least, not to me. The threat was always more than enough. But my brother Reese swears Mom showed his old girlfriend the picture of him dressed up as a sheep for the school Christmas play. And Gina actually burned her baby pictures to avoid the threat altogether. Mom's still pretty ticked off about that."

Daisy chuckled, but a part of her worried. Listening to him, she knew just how important a child's memories of his mother were. And there was so much she didn't know about being a mother. How would she have learned? She'd never had a role model. No one to watch. What if she messed it all up? What if she was so terrible at this whole motherhood thing that she ended up scarring poor Angel for life?

"Okay, that story was supposed to make you smile."

"It's just…" She walked around to the front of the stroller, squatted in front of it and smoothed the baby's blanket. Her tiny daughter's vulnerability struck her hard, and Daisy heard herself wonder aloud. "What if I suck at this?"

"At what?"

"At being her mother."

"You won't."

She tipped her head back to look up at him, and studied his face. "And since you've known me for a few weeks, you can assure me of this…how?"

Alex crouched beside her and met her gaze dead-on, with a seriousness that sent a shiver straight to the center of her soul.

"Because I've known you for a few weeks."

Covering her hand with his, he gave her fingers a quick squeeze and somehow managed to take a grip on her heart, too. She looked into those dark brown eyes and felt herself drift just a little deeper into the warmth she saw there.

"Sometimes," he was saying, "you can meet someone and in a few days know them better than others you might have known for years." He pulled his hand back and smiled at her. "I know you, Daisy Cusak. You *are* a good mother."

"There hasn't been a whole lot of mothering to judge me on yet."

He shook his head slowly and smiled. "Every time you touch her, it shows. Besides, the first tip-off is bad mothers don't worry about if they're good at it or not."

She wanted to believe him. She wanted to be everything her daughter would ever need. But she couldn't be. Even the best mom couldn't be a daddy. And the thought that someday Angel might feel cheated because she didn't have a father was enough to rattle Daisy. Then thoughts of the years to come and all of the things that she would have to handle alone sent a cold chill rolling along her spine.

In her stroller, Angel twisted, kicked at her soft, pale green blanket, waved her tiny fists in the air and tugged at her mother's heart all at the same time. Whatever she needed, Daisy would find a way to provide it. She might make mistakes in raising her, but it wouldn't be for lack of trying.

"So," Alex asked, giving Daisy a smile that curled her toes and set tiny flames whispering through her bloodstream, "are you ready to take your first step into motherhood and start building that blackmail file?''

"Yes," she said, "I think I am." Besides, she wanted to remember today. This day spent with Alex, when the three of them had felt so much like a family.

Eight

"**I** don't see what the big problem is." Daisy's waitress friend Joan smiled down at the baby, cradled in the crook of her arm. While she talked to Daisy, she kept grinning and making silly faces at Angel. "I mean, geez, we should all have such terrible ordeals to live through. A rich, handsome man wants to spend time with you. Why don't you go step out in front of a truck and end the misery?"

"Very funny." Daisy folded Angel's laundry and set it in a neat stack beside her on the couch. Joan had stopped by on her way in to work the lunch shift at Antonio's. And she hadn't stopped talking about Alex yet.

Late morning sunshine poured in from the single window overlooking the back alley. It wasn't much of a view, but with her window box filled with determinedly cheerful yellow and orange nasturtiums, Daisy could fool herself into thinking she had a lovely garden just outside. The faded, overstuffed furniture was comfortable and welcoming, and just being here, in the nest she'd built for herself, gave her a feeling of warm satisfaction.

Which Joan was trying to shake up.

"Well, come on." Her friend made big eyes at the baby. "You tell her, Angel. Tell Mommy to just chill out and enjoy herself already."

"Easy for you to say," Daisy countered. It had been nearly a week since that day in the mall when she and Angel had posed for their first picture together. And in that week, Alex had become even more of a regular visitor than he had been before. He would show up carrying a pizza, or a couple of videos or Chinese food or… Daisy shook her head. She just didn't know what was coming next. And that was part of the problem. She liked knowing. She liked having a plan. Being able to see far enough down the road in front of her so that there were no surprises.

Unfortunately, around Alex she'd discovered way too many bends in the road to be able to see very far at all.

Joan slowly sank onto the other end of the sofa,

curled her legs up under her and shifted Angel to her other arm. "I just don't get it. Why does this bug you so much? Do you hate the guy?" As soon as she said the words, Joan's face clouded up and her eyes narrowed in suspicion. "Hey, is that it? Do you want him to leave you alone and he's not? Is he like a stalker or something? 'Cause if he is, I'll talk to Big Mike at the restaurant and he'll—"

"No!" Daisy spoke up so quickly it startled the baby, who jumped in Joan's arms. Guiltily, Daisy lowered her voice again. "It's not like that. And for heaven's sake, I don't need Big Mike." Just the thought of the two hundred fifty pound wrestler-turned-waiter was enough to make Daisy smile. He looked so big and mean, yet was as protective of the waitresses as a mother hen with her chicks.

Sighing, she leaned back, still clutching a tiny pink T-shirt. "The problem isn't that I *don't* like him. It's that I *do*."

"Then I repeat—chill out and enjoy."

"I can't."

"Why the hell not?"

To Joan these things were black-and-white. But then, Joan didn't have to worry about a baby, did she? Yet even as that defense went through her mind, Daisy had to discount it. It wasn't Angel keeping her from making more of Alex's attentions than she was. This was all Daisy. She'd trusted a man once—and he'd left her alone and pregnant.

Not that she thought Alex was that kind of guy. But then she hadn't thought Jeff was, either. Had she?

"I know what you're thinking."

Daisy sighed. "Suddenly everybody's a mind reader."

"Huh?"

"Nothing. Go on. What am I thinking?"

"You're comparing Alex Barone to that worthless, lying, no good, lazy, shiftless..." she paused and covered Angel's ears with her hands, so the baby wouldn't hear her father's name "...Jeff."

"No, I'm not."

"No?"

"All right, maybe I am. A little. Do you blame me?"

"I guess not," Joan admitted, sitting back against the cushions and staring down into Angel's eyes. "But, honey, all men aren't like that louse. Are you going to join a convent because of one creep?"

"I don't think convents take single mothers."

"Their loss."

Daisy smiled, in spite of the weird conversation. She'd always been able to count on Joan for just about anything. She'd been a good friend over the last few years. And she understood what Daisy had gone through after Jeff left. But Joan came from a warm, loving family. She had parents, two brothers who teased her unmercifully, and nephews and nieces, and she had no idea what it was like to be completely alone. To have no one for support when your legs got knocked out from under you.

Daisy just couldn't risk being hurt that badly again. Not when it would affect Angel this time, too.

Joan glanced at her wristwatch, sucked in a breath and reluctantly laid Angel down on the wide sofa cushions. "I'm gonna be late. Gotta go."

"Say hi to everyone for me."

"I will." She slung her brown leather shoulder bag onto her left arm, straightened her short, black uniform skirt, then said, "You know I'm on your side, right?"

"Sure I know that."

"Okay. Just checking." Waving one hand at Daisy to tell her to keep her seat, Joan headed for the door. But she paused with one hand on the doorknob. "You know," she said with a smile, looking back over her shoulder, "if you decide you really don't want him hanging around, you could always throw him my way."

"I'll keep it in mind," Daisy said wryly. But after Joan left, Daisy realized that the thought of Alex Barone with someone else made her stomach churn.

And that told her she was in big trouble.

Alex left his parents' Beacon Hill town house and hurried down the walk toward the street. Late morning sunlight poured over the city in a pale warning of the summer heat lurking just around the corner. Soon enough the city would be steaming under a blanket of humidity. But for now, there was a breeze drifting in off the ocean and the promise of another day spent with Daisy and the baby.

Behind him, he heard the front door open and close again quickly. The rapid click of heels on the walk told him who was chasing him even before he turned around to say, "What is it, Rita? I'm in a hurry."

"Yeah," his younger sister said. "I noticed."

Squinting in the sunlight, he let out a hiss of impatience. He'd cut short his visit with his parents for a reason. And that reason was waiting for him in a tiny apartment on the other side of town. "What's that supposed to mean?"

Rita dismissed his irritation as only a sister could. "I mean, you've hardly seen the family since you've been back in town. You've been spending all your time with Daisy, haven't you?"

A teenager on a skateboard shouted "Heads up!" and barreled toward them along the sidewalk.

Alex grabbed his sister's arm and pulled her out of range. Then, leaning back against the SUV he'd rented a few days ago, he watched her for a long minute before saying, "That's none of your business, Rita."

"Family's family."

"And who I see is up to me."

"I know that." A breeze whipped her hair across her eyes and she plucked it away to stare up at him. "Don't get me wrong, I like Daisy."

"Then what's this about?"

She shrugged and shoved both hands into the pockets of her jeans. "Look, Alex, Daisy's a sweetie. I know that. But she's a single mom with a lot to deal with right now."

"And?"

"And you're a guy who's on his way out of town."

"Not for another three weeks."

"Oh, well then, never mind."

Impatience tugged at him, but Alex knew his family well enough to realize he wouldn't be going anywhere until Rita had said what she wanted to.

"Say what you came out here to say, all right?"

"Fine. Daisy doesn't need you pretending to be Prince Charming before you fuel up your jet and fly off into the sunset."

"What am I supposed to do?" he demanded. "Not see her? Stay away?"

Rita looked up at him and he saw understanding and sympathy in her eyes. Neither of which appealed to him at the moment. "If you're just going to walk away from her in three weeks, then yeah."

"And if I'm not going to walk away?" The words were out before he could censor them. He'd been doing a lot of thinking lately, and most especially, he'd been thinking about having to leave Daisy. Hell, a few weeks ago he hadn't known she existed. Now he woke up every morning eager to see her. Wanting to be with her, near her. He wanted to touch her. Wanted to kiss her, hold her and have her turn to him in the night. He wanted to belong in that tiny apartment with the rain forest look to it. That cozy sense of warmth she created wherever she was drew him in and made him want more.

And the thought of leaving her in three weeks made him almost regret, for the first time, being in the military.

Rita smiled up at him. "Could this be it?"

He frowned at her. "It what?"

But she didn't answer. She just chuckled, shook her head and muttered, "I never would have believed it."

"What're you talking about?"

"Not a thing, big brother," she said, and rose up on her toes to plant a kiss on his cheek. "Not a single thing." Then she turned and headed back to the house, leaving Alex staring after her, wondering why women had to be so damned confusing.

"I said, you've made a mistake." Daisy kept one hand on the doorjamb and the other on the door itself, ready to slam it shut and lock it, just in case. It paid to be careful anyway, but when you were dealing with a surly deliveryman who had to weigh three hundred pounds...

"Look, lady," he muttered, waving his clipboard at her again, as if it were a magic wand and this time he'd be able to make her change her mind. "It says right here—deliver to Daisy Cusak. You Daisy?"

"Yes, but..."

"Last name Cusak?"

She huffed out a breath. "Yes."

"Then we don't got a problem, do we?" He stared down at her through two steely-blue eyes set in a wide, weatherworn face. Clearly, he expected her to back up and let him in with whatever was stacked behind him in the narrow hallway.

Daisy was not going to comply.

"There *is* a problem because I didn't order anything and I'm—"

"I ordered it," said a voice from the hall. A familiar voice. One that had the ability to trail along her skin like silk.

"Alex?" She tried to peer past the boxes and the mountain of man standing between her and the hall. But she wasn't about to let go of that door. Not yet.

"I'm here." In another second or two, he appeared, squeezing between two huge boxes and the big man who was growing more surly by the minute.

"What's this about?" she asked as Alex stepped into the apartment. He took her arm and moved her out of the way, while opening the door wider at the same time.

"Just a sec," he said. Then to the deliveryman he said, "Just bring it inside. I'll take it from there."

"Okay by me," the fellow said, giving Daisy a look that told her he was thankful that at last a *man* had arrived to clear things up.

"Alex," she demanded as she watched a stranger set two big boxes and several smaller ones down in the middle of her already cramped living room, "what is going on?"

He just grinned, dipped into his jeans pocket for his wallet and pulled out a couple of bills. Handing them to the man, he said, "Thanks," and let him out, closing the door behind him.

Once they were alone again, Alex glanced around the room. "Where's the baby?"

"She's asleep."

"Good."

He looked so pleased with himself. A slow smile curved his mouth and seemed to reach across the room to light a small fire in her belly. She deliberately tamped it out. Hormones. It was just hormones.

"Alex, what are you doing?"

"It's a surprise."

"Yeah, so far." She glanced down at the unopened cartons and back again to him. "What is all this stuff?"

"I went shopping." He shrugged, then dropped to his knees beside the biggest box. Reaching into his pocket, he pulled out a small knife, opened it up and slit the cardboard.

"For what?" She stepped to the side, so she could keep an eye on both him and the box.

"You'll see." When he had the strapping tape cut away, he tossed the lid of the box aside and said, "Ta-da."

Daisy looked down and saw a disassembled crib. Frowning, she shifted her gaze to him. "A crib? Angel already has a crib."

"I know," he said, then pulled some of the packing paper away from the intricately carved, pale oak headboard. "But this is the Cadillac of baby furniture."

She was sure it was. The thing was gorgeous, and compared to the secondhand crib she'd painstakingly painted herself, it looked even better. And apparently Alex thought Angel deserved more than her mother could provide. Which stung Daisy more than she wanted to admit.

She'd been taking care of herself for a long time. She didn't need a rich, handsome prince riding to her rescue.

As he pulled piece after piece out of the carton and she stood there, silently watching, Daisy felt her control slipping away. The shiny new crib made her whole apartment look different. Instead of cozy and familiar, the furniture now looked a little shabby. Forlorn. She'd always taken pride in the home she'd made for herself. But now she was seeing it as Alex must see it.

And she didn't like it one bit.

"Take it back."

"What?"

"I mean it, Alex. Take it back." She moved away from the carton and him. "Angel already has a bed. We don't need this."

Obviously confused, he said, "I know you don't *need* it. I just wanted you to have it."

"Why?"

"Huh?"

"Why? It's a simple question."

He set the crib aside and stood up to face her.

"Because I saw it and I thought, apparently wrongly, that it would make you happy."

"Because what I can give her isn't enough?"

"That's not what this is about." His voice dropped a notch or two, and she heard a thread of anger rising through it.

Damn it, since when was giving someone a present a capital offense? For the first time ever, Alex had dipped into the inheritance he'd come into when he turned twenty-one. Until now, he'd been content to live on his salary as a navy pilot. It was only for Daisy and Angel that he'd wanted more.

And hadn't that turned out well?

"I'm not spending time with you because you're a Barone, you know."

"I know." He threw his hands up, then let them slap against his thighs. Where was this coming from?

"I don't care if you're rich."

"My family's rich. I'm a pilot."

"Whatever. I'm not interested in your family's money."

"I never said you were."

"Then why would you do all of this without even talking to me first?"

He crossed the room to her in three angry strides. Damn it, he'd wanted to help. To make her smile. To do something nice for a woman he was pretty sure didn't experience that very often. And if he said all that to her, he had the distinct feeling she might punch him.

"I was downtown, picking something up for my mother, when I looked in a window and saw this crib."

Her gaze fixed on him, waiting.

"And like an idiot, I thought you'd like it. I thought it would be a nice surprise." He grabbed hold of her shoulders and ignored the flash of heat that swept from her body straight into his. "I love Angel. Like she was mine. I wanted to do something nice for her before I shipped out. Okay?"

That wasn't all of it. That wasn't nearly all. He'd

wanted to make Daisy smile. To see her eyes sparkle with delight. To be the one to make her happy.

Idiot.

"You don't have to spend your money on us, Alex."

"Yeah," he snapped, letting her go and turning around to pack up the crib again. "You know, I noticed that there was nobody holding a gun to my head, forcing me to buy these things."

"I just don't know what to do here," Daisy said softly, and he looked over his shoulder at her. "Nobody's ever... Well, I mean..."

"You could say thank you."

"I could." She took a step closer to him.

Alex stood stock-still, not wanting to break the connection that held them.

When she was less than an arm's reach away, she went up on her toes and gave him a quick, light kiss on the cheek. "Thank you."

He ground his teeth together and fisted his hands at his sides to keep from reaching for her. He wanted nothing more than to yank her close, wrap his arms around her and kiss her until neither of them could breathe. But the moment was too tenuous for that. And she'd given him no sign at all that she was interested in him as anything other than a friend.

Well, he wasn't about to trust his heart again to a woman who didn't want it. He'd learned that lesson the hard way. So he fought down his own instincts, his hunger, and said simply, "You're welcome."

They were so close he could feel her breath and count the beats of her heart, throbbing at the base of her throat. He wanted her more than anything. He spent his days being her friend and his nights dreaming about being her lover.

And neither situation was good enough.

He wanted more.

For both of them.

But if Daisy hadn't wanted the gifts he'd brought her, why would she want him?

Nine

Daisy couldn't even remember a time when Alex wasn't a part of her life. He'd made a place for himself so neatly, so quietly, she hadn't seen it coming, and hadn't been able to defend herself against it—even if she'd wanted to. Which, she admitted, she probably wouldn't have.

It was crazy. It was completely out of the realm of reality. She was a fool to let herself get used to him being there. But at the same time, she just couldn't bring herself to stop enjoying it.

Strange, but up until the night Alex had walked into her life, she'd considered herself happy. She'd had her job, her home, her baby to plan for, and had routinely counted her blessings. Now, though, she was beginning to want more. Even knowing that she didn't have a snowball's chance in hell of that dream ever coming true.

Lying in her bed, Daisy stared up at the ceiling and tried to ignore the ache deep within. It was ridiculous to be so stirred up inside when the man hadn't done anything to deliberately raise her blood pressure. But then, apparently just being around him was enough to make her tremble with a need she hadn't felt in far too long.

Tossing the blankets back, Daisy swung her legs off the bed and stood up. She wasn't going to get any sleep, so she might as well get up and do something. Anything. Keep busy so her brain wouldn't conjure up images of Alex's eyes. His mouth. His hands.

"Oh, boy."

She walked into the baby's room and by the glow of a fairy princess night-light, crossed the room to stand beside the brand-new crib. Daisy stared down at her daughter, peacefully sleeping, and envied the infant her untroubled dreams. She ran one hand over the cool, smooth oak railing and thought about Alex's hands putting this bed together. How they'd laughed over the practically unreadable instructions, and how proud he'd been to install his gift in the baby's room.

"And this isn't helping," she whispered firmly to

herself. Turning around, she left the room, keeping the door open so she could hear Angel's slightest cry, and walked into the living room. She flicked on a light and, on automatic pilot, cruised the small area, straightening pillows, picking up papers, looking for something to keep herself occupied. Something to draw her attention away from the man who never seemed to leave her thoughts.

But it was a losing battle and she knew it. Even after Alex had gone and their time together was nothing more than a memory, she'd remember him. She knew that during the long nights in the years to come, her brain would torture her by replaying the events of the past few weeks. Every time she looked into her daughter's face, she would remember the night of her birth and the feel of Alex's hand on hers.

A knock on the door startled her, and Daisy's gaze flew to the nearby clock. Eleven o'clock. Who would be coming by at this time of night?

She hurried across the living room and looked through the peephole in the door. Alex. Her body jumped to life and even her blood seemed to be doing somersaults in her veins. It was as if her thoughts had conjured him, and surrendering to fate, she threw the chain off and opened the door.

Alex just stared at her for a long minute. Soft, chestnut-brown hair tumbled around her face. Her shoulders were bare beneath the straps of her powder-blue tank top, and the thin material skimmed her small, perfect breasts, outlining her peaked nipples just enough to taunt him. Worn white boxer shorts hung loosely around her narrow waist and hips, displaying a swatch of pale skin that made him want to touch her and relish the smoothness of her flesh. Pink polish decorated her toenails and she wore a silver toe ring on her left foot. She looked warm and rumpled and ready for loving.

The only thing that held him in place was the fact that he knew that, medically speaking, she wasn't ready.

She stepped back to let him in and he moved quickly, before she could change her mind. Man, he was in bad shape.

"Alex, what are you doing here?"

"I was outside. In my car. I saw your light come on...." He paused. "Great. Now I sound like a stalker." He scraped one hand across the top of his head, then shoved that hand into his jeans pocket. "I know how that sounds and I don't like it any better than you do. But for some reason, I just..." He shrugged, as if silently admitting he couldn't come up with a good reason for being there. "I just got in my car and I ended up here."

What he didn't admit to was that being with his friends hadn't taken his mind off Daisy. That sitting in a bar having a beer wasn't any fun when all he really wanted to do was be with her. Damn it, he hadn't counted on this.

He'd sworn off love. Being dumped on Valentine's Day shortly before your wedding did that to a man. But Daisy had slipped beneath his radar. She'd come up on him on his blind side, and by the time he'd noticed just how deeply she'd crawled under his skin, it was too late.

Now he didn't want to be rid of her. Now he just wanted to be *inside* her.

Everything in him went hot and still at the thought, and it took every ounce of his self-control to keep from grabbing her.

"I'm glad," she said, and shattered that self-control in an instant.

Alex stepped close to her, wrapped his arms around her and pulled her against him. He felt the small, rigid tips of her nipples pressing into his chest, and he deliberately shifted her, rubbing her flesh against him until he saw her eyes go soft and cloudy.

"You just had a baby," he whispered, his right hand sweeping down her back to glide over the curve of her behind.

"Mmm…"

"I don't want to hurt you."

"You're not," she said, and gasped slightly as his left hand came around and slid between their bodies to cup her breast.

Alex's gaze moved over her features slowly, deliberately, enjoying the rush of color in her pale cheeks, and the way her lips parted with a sigh of desire. The quiet in the room seemed to close in on them, taking them out of the world into a place where only the two of them existed.

"I want you, Daisy," he murmured. The admission stirred his blood into a thick, boiling mass of need.

Her eyes opened wide and she looked up at him, tilting her head back. The line of her neck tempted him to lay a string of hot, damp kisses on her flesh. His thumb moved over the tip of her nipple and she flinched, inhaling sharply, deeply.

"I know," she said. "I feel it, too."

Those few words acted like a bellows on the fire in his gut, fanning the flames until he felt consumed by them. This was why he'd come here so late at night. This was why his friends' chatter had sounded like an annoying hum of noise. With Daisy in his mind, his blood, he could think of nothing else.

"I need to kiss you. I've been thinking about it all night," he told her.

"I have, too. Couldn't sleep. Couldn't think."

"There's no thinking anymore," he murmured. "Just feeling. Tasting."

When she licked her lips, the quick dart of her tongue nearly undid him. Need crouched inside him like some caged tiger waiting for the chance to pounce. He'd never felt this before. This all-consuming urgency to be with someone. To feel that someone close and warm and eager.

In the soft lamplight, he watched her as he lowered his head to hers. Slowly, deliberately, drawing out the pleasure, the anticipation of that first brush of lips to lips. And when he couldn't stand the suspense another instant, he took her mouth with his.

Electrical.

Fiery.

Sizzling.

Heat blistered between them, and a kiss that began as a soft, teasing caress became a feast fit for a starving man. Alex's arms came around her, pinning her to him with a strength he kept carefully in check even as he held her tightly enough that there was no chance of her escaping him, had she wanted to.

But she threw her arms around his neck and hung on just as tightly to him, as though he were the only stable force in the universe. If that was so, then the world was in serious trouble, he thought, because he felt as though he was teetering on the edge of a chasm.

And in the next instant, he jumped in willingly and dragged her along with him.

Alex parted her lips with a swipe of his tongue and delved into the warm, damp heat of her. He groaned at the hard, sweet relief of having her mouth on his. He tasted her, reveling in the hot, thick pumping of his blood and the eager response from her. She gave as good as she got, and stole his breath with her reaction to his kiss. She molded herself to him, leaning into his body, pressing hard along the length of him.

He tightened his arms around her, lifting her feet right off the floor. Her small, compact body felt so right against his. This was where they'd been headed since that first night at Antonio's. A part of him had known it then, when he'd looked into her eyes and lost himself in the glory of her.

Their tongues mated, dancing, entwining, stroking, caressing. His hands moved up and down her back, following the line of her curves, feeling her lush body come alive beneath his touch. He skimmed his hands under the hem of her shirt, wanting, needing to feel her, skin to skin. She sighed into his mouth as his fingers trailed along her spine. His body tightened even more and he took her mouth harder, deeper, wanting to give and take all he could. He needed this time with Daisy to feed the fires that had started burning within him weeks ago.

His hands slipped beneath the loose waistband of her shorts and swept across her behind, loving the feel of her soft, cool flesh. His fingertips hummed with an electrical force that seemed to send the tingling sensation deep inside him, where it obliterated every thought but the need to feel more. To touch more. She shifted in his arms, moving even closer until he thought she just might slide right inside him. Still that wouldn't be close enough. Not for him.

And not for Daisy.

At his touch, she melted.

That was the only word swimming through her mind. Alex's touch was like nothing she'd ever experienced before. It was as if thunder and lightning were pounding through her body, and she was awash in a storm that kept building until she was afraid she wouldn't be able to breathe. Somehow she didn't care, so long as he kept touching her.

She moved against him and his hands swept over her behind, cupping her, pulling her close enough to him that she felt the hard, thick proof of his desire pressing into her belly. Damp heat roared through her and her knees weakened, so she leaned into him farther, trusting him to keep her upright.

Magic, she thought. It was magic that a man's touch could be so exciting. So all-consuming that nothing else mattered but the next touch. And the next.

She hadn't counted on this. Hadn't known she could ever feel this. Every cell in her body felt more alive than ever before.

When he tore his mouth from hers, she wanted to moan in disappointment, but he only lowered his head to kiss her neck, her throat. He clamped his mouth to the pulse beat at the base of her throat, and she felt her heart quicken in answer to the touch of his tongue to her already sensitized skin. She clutched his shoulders, digging her fingers into the soft fabric of his dark red T-shirt, and leaned back, silently pleading for his lips to go lower, farther. She wanted his mouth on her breasts, wanted to feel the heat of him pressed close to her heart.

"Too many clothes," he whispered, his breath dusting her skin like drops of fire from a sparkler.

"Yes," she agreed, wanting nothing between them right now. Not even the flimsy barrier of fabric.

His hands swept up, under the hem of her tank top, and in seconds, he'd pulled it off over her head to leave her breasts naked to his touch.

The cool air brushed her skin, making her nipples pucker tighter, harder. She shivered, but not from cold. It was Alex's gaze locked on her breasts that sent a tremor rippling throughout her body.

"Beautiful," he said, his hands skimming across her breasts, pausing long enough to tweak her nipples with a gentle pressure designed to drive her insane. "You're beautiful, Daisy," he said. "More beautiful than I'd thought."

She didn't feel beautiful.

She felt on fire.

She felt as though, if he didn't kiss her and touch her, she would erupt into a ball of flame and burn out right before his eyes. Her skin prickled. Her mouth went dry as she looked into his deep-brown eyes and saw an answering fire there.

"Touch me, Alex," she said with a sigh that came from her soul. "I want to feel your hands on me."

And then he growled, low in his throat, and the deep, rumbling sound rolled along her spine, causing goose bumps and making her body feel even more sensitive, more alive than before.

He picked her up, sweeping her into his arms, and carried her to the couch. There he sat down with her across his lap, and Daisy squirmed slightly, feeling his body tight and hard beneath hers and wishing she could have him inside her.

Laying her back until her head hung over the arm of the sofa, Alex bent down to take first one nipple and then the other into his mouth.

Daisy arched into him, nearly jumping right off the couch. Then she relaxed and sighed at the wonder of his mouth on her body. His tongue, his lips, his teeth tormented her, driving her need higher and higher until all she could do was lie helplessly in his grasp and try to remember to breathe.

He touched her again, letting his right hand sweep across her belly, his fingertips dancing lightly against her skin, building a fire that needed no stoking. She closed her eyes and concentrated on the sensations coursing through her. It had been so long since she'd felt cherished. Since she'd had someone hold her, kiss her. Even then, it had been nothing like this. Nothing.

Alex was a law unto himself. He touched her and there was brilliant light. He took his hand away and there was darkness.

And she wanted the light.

Wanted the fire.

Wanted the crashing blow of a release she knew was waiting just out of her reach.

His fingers dipped again beneath the waistband of her shorts and skimmed lightly down her belly until he found his target.

Daisy lifted her head, struggled for air and looked at him as his mouth worked her nipples, as his hand poised to begin the final assault on her nerves. She took a gasping breath and held it. He cupped her. She groaned tightly, closed her eyes and clutched his shoulders again as her hips arched off his lap and rocked wildly, impatiently.

Need simmered inside her, and she nearly whimpered with desire.

A part of him knew there'd be no satisfaction for him tonight. It was too soon for her. Too soon after having the baby. So he would find his pleasure in satisfying her. To touch her like this, to feel her excitement, her surrender, was like a drug. He lapped it up and wanted more. He suckled her harder, deeper, until he was sure he felt her spirit enter his soul.

And then he touched her.

His fingertips found her center, damp and hot and ready. The first time he stroked her, she trembled in his arms and gave a muffled moan that tore at him and fed the hunger within. Still he wanted more. Wanted to *give* more. Because for the first time in his life, giving satisfaction was like receiving it. He felt each of her tremors. Felt the fire building. Felt the need crowding close. Felt the race toward completion. And he pushed her faster, harder, wanting to feel her release ripple through her and into him.

Sliding one arm under her back, he pulled her close and lifted his head to watch her face. He relished each moan, savored each whimper. Her hips moved, rocking her body against his hand as he took her swiftly toward the peak of pleasure.

"Look at me," he whispered, his voice raspy with need. "Daisy, look at me."

Even lost in the hazy world of passion, she heard him and responded. Her eyes opened and her gaze met his and locked on.

"I want to watch you," he said softly, and leaned forward to kiss her briefly, tenderly.

"Alex…" Her breath caught and she moved in his arms again, struggling toward release.

"Let go, Daisy. Let go and fall," he urged, whispering against her mouth, keeping his gaze on hers, wanting to see the completion fill those soft blue eyes. "I'll catch you. Let go."

"Alex, I—" Her breath hitched. She stared into his eyes and he saw the first flash of wonder splinter her gaze. Her body quaked, trembled. She gasped, arched high into his embrace and moaned his name as she fell blindly into the chasm where he waited to catch her.

Ten

The very moment her body stopped quivering, Daisy took a long, deep breath and brought her arms up to cover her breasts. A little late, she knew, but somehow, now that the firestorm was over, she felt just a bit underdressed.

One corner of Alex's mouth twitched. "I have to tell you, locking that barn door isn't gonna bring the horse back."

"Maybe not," she said, "but I feel better with the doors closed." She sat up, then immediately stilled when he hissed in a breath. Daisy was suddenly all too aware of his hard-as-steel body beneath her. "Umm…"

"Just sit still, okay?"

"Maybe it'd be better if I got off your lap."

"Better for whom?" he asked. "I'm sort of enjoying this."

"What are you, a masochist?" A smile twitched her lips. "You know I can't..."

He let a groan escape him even as he held her firmly in place. "Yeah. I know."

Daisy just stared at him. He knew she couldn't have sex with him, and yet he'd just stirred things up between them to the point where if she hadn't found release, she would have exploded. He must feel the same way. "Then why—"

He slid one hand up her spine to cup the back of her head, his fingers spearing through the soft tangle of her hair. "Because I had to touch you. I had to kiss you."

She turned her head, feeling his touch against her scalp and savoring the heat tumbling through her bloodstream.

"It's been driving me nuts for weeks, Daisy," he said, his voice tight and harsh with the need still strangling him. His fingers tightened on her hair and he pulled her head closer until her mouth was just a breath away from his. "All I could think about was you. Being with you, being close to you."

Daisy's insides did a quick flip and twist. She stared into his eyes and wondered how she'd lived twenty-six years without being able to see them. To see the richness and the warmth shining there. And then she wondered how in the world she would live through the rest of her life *without* seeing them.

When this little interlude was over and he'd shipped out, she'd never be able to sit on this sofa again without remembering the feel of his hands on her body. She'd never be able to come into this apartment at all without expecting to hear the sound of his voice or see his smile. And what she was going to do about that, she didn't have a clue.

But for now, she enjoyed his hands on her body and forgot about her brush with embarrassment. Forgot about everything but the feel of him touching her. Wrapping her arms around his neck, she kissed him slowly, deeply, tenderly, showing him without words just how much it meant to be in the circle of his arms.

And when the kiss was over and she pulled back to look at him, she saw him smile despite the ache glittering in his eyes. He'd taken her higher, faster and further than anyone ever had. He'd shown her magic and had never thought of his own misery. But she was. And suddenly she wanted to give him the same gift he'd given her.

"But now," Daisy said softly, cupping his face with her hands, "can't I do something for you?"

He reached up and covered her hands with his own. Turning his face slightly, he kissed her palm. "No."

"Why no?"

"Because I can wait. I want you, Daisy, but I'll wait until I can have all of you."

No promise of love or forever. But then, she hadn't expected them, had she? He wanted her, and at least that was honest.

Her stomach swirled with nerves and expectation, and a brand-new flash of desire simmered even hotter than before. Now she knew what she could find with him. Now she was aware of what his touch could do to her body, her soul. And the thought of waiting to experience it all again was almost more than she could bear.

For now, he was hers. For now, she had the magic. The sensation of being in the arms of a man she'd never thought she'd find.

And she was going to enjoy it for however long it lasted.

She'd mourn its loss when it was over.

When she was alone.

"You're worth the wait," he said, pulling her to him to rest against his chest.

She listened to the thundering beat of his heart and told herself to remember it all.

Remember it for the time when he was just a memory.

And the nights were too long and too lonely.

The next week crawled by.

Alex felt as though he was balanced on a sword's

razor edge. That one night with Daisy was on permanent rewind in his brain. He saw it all over and over again. He felt her silky skin, heard her soft moans and experienced her tremors as completely as he had then. And it tortured him, knowing that he couldn't have her again.

Not yet, anyway.

"Damn, Barone," Mike Hannigan nearly shouted. "Where the hell are you?"

"Huh?"

"She must be something else," his friend said with a shake of his head.

"She who?"

"She whoever's taking up all of your brain space."

Thunder rolled and crashed in the distance, and Alex reached for his beer. The other guys were bowling another round, but he and Mike were sitting this game out. Around him, people laughed and talked. From the bar came the slow swell of blues blasting from speakers. Kids scattered at the door to the video game room like marbles shot out of a circle.

Alex just looked at his friend for a long minute. "It's Daisy."

Mike frowned thoughtfully, then his expression cleared again. "The pregnant waitress from the restaurant?"

"Not pregnant anymore, and yes."

Mike picked up his beer and leaned back in the booth. Taking a long sip, he swallowed, then studied the label on the bottle. "This serious?"

When Alex didn't say anything, Mike hooted a laugh. "Who woulda thought it? Babe Magnet Barone, off the market?"

Babe magnet. The guys were always giving him grief about how easily he met women. And for the most part, they were right. He'd never had trouble finding a woman to kill a few hours—or a few weeks, with. He'd only sucked at finding the one *right* woman. Which was why he'd sworn off even looking, for the last couple of years.

Until Daisy.

Was he off the market now? Hell, he didn't know. God knew he cared for Daisy more than he had ever cared for anyone else. Even what he'd felt for his former fiancée didn't compare to this. But that didn't make it real. Didn't promise happily ever after.

Besides, Daisy was stubborn. Proud. Hell, she even fought him when he tried to give her gifts. When she talked about her plans, the future she hoped to make for herself and Angel, he wasn't a part of them. Maybe she was already trying to close him out of her life.

Except for one heavy petting session, his and Daisy's relationship had been nothing but friendly. So if he were interested in something a little

more…intimate, who was to say that she would be?
He'd believed in a woman before, and all it got him
was a slightly used engagement ring and a lot of
unwanted condolences from sympathetic friends and
family.

Just the thought of that was enough to make him
take a mental step back from wherever his brain was
starting to lead him.

"Are you in love with her?" Mike asked, and the
question fought its way through the fog in Alex's
brain.

He thought about that for a long minute or two,
trying to put a name to his feelings. But it was as
elusive as the emotions themselves. "I don't
know," he said finally.

"Well hell, boy," Mike told him. "You've got
about fifteen days of leave left to figure it out."

Alex picked up his beer and took a long swig.
The last few weeks had gone by so fast, he'd hardly
noticed. But Mike was right. Leave time was almost
up.

Fifteen days. Then he'd be out of here. Back on
duty and shipped to who knew where for who knew
how long. Usually, the thought of getting back into
the cockpit of a navy jet was enough to cheer Alex
right up.

So how come now it sounded more like a sen-
tence?

* * *

A few days later, Rita smiled and waved to Daisy as she and the baby approached the sidewalk café.

"Oh my God," Rita exclaimed as she jumped from her chair to scoop Angel out of her stroller for a closer examination. "I can't believe how big she is."

Daisy smiled proudly as her daughter was cooed over. Time was moving fast. Angel was becoming her own person now, more aware of her world and the people in it. She lit up like a Christmas tree when Daisy came into the room—but when she saw Alex, the baby reacted as if Santa himself had shown up.

And what would she think when Alex stopped coming to see her? Would she miss him? Would she even notice? Yes, Daisy thought, wincing slightly at the twinge of pain that gripped her heart. Angel would notice his absence. But no more than Daisy would.

Since that one night on her sofa, things between her and Alex had become even more strained. As time ticked past, both of them knew that soon she'd be physically ready to make love again. But the real question was, was she *emotionally* ready?

Her feelings for Alex were already so confusing she knew that the moment she slept with him, her brain would short-circuit.

"She's a beauty," Rita was saying, and Daisy steeled her mind against thoughts of Alex. At least for a while.

"Thank you. And thank you again for delivering her. I really don't know what I would have done if you hadn't helped me that night." Daisy took a seat opposite Rita at the table. Smoothing the skirt of her pale green outfit, Daisy was glad she'd taken the time to dress up a bit. Her usual choice of jeans and a T-shirt would have been decidedly out of place at the tiny, but exclusive restaurant.

"Oh," Rita said, cuddling Angel in the crook of her arm, "you'd have managed. Mother Nature would have kicked in and taken charge."

"I'm still glad I had you to help me." In one incredible night, Daisy had forged a bond with Rita, Maria and Alex. And that connection to the Barone family made her feel almost as if she belonged. Which was a lovely feeling—even if it was pretty much a fantasy.

Rita smiled and smoothed the tip of one well-manicured finger along the baby's cheek. "It was my pleasure. Heck, I've been bragging about that little adventure for nearly six weeks."

The waiter came, dropped their menus on the table, then walked away again, giving them a few minutes to talk.

"And speaking of six weeks," Rita said, "I know this is nosy, but I'm a nurse. I can't help myself. Have you been to see your doctor?"

"Tomorrow," Daisy said, and a swirl of emotion fluttered through her in a haze of brilliant colors and breath-stealing heat. Once she got the all-clear from her doctor, there'd be nothing standing between her and Alex sleeping together.

Was that a good thing? Or a bad thing?

"Seen Alex lately?"

"Hmm?" Don't blush at the sound of his name, for pity's sake.

"Alex," Rita prodded with a wry grin. "My brother. Big guy? Good-looking?"

Daisy smiled and took the baby from Rita long enough to settle her into the stroller. The stalling tactic also gave her an extra second or two to compose herself before having to speak again. After all, she didn't want to drool in front of the man's sister. "Yeah, I know who you mean."

"Just checking."

"I saw him yesterday." Daisy sat up straight again and took a deep breath.

"You've been seeing him a lot."

"Sort of," Daisy said, not really sure where this was going.

Rita laughed and picked up her menu. "Relax, Daisy. It's not an inquisition. I'd just like to get to know my brother's girlfriend better, that's all."

"I'm not—"

"Yeah, yeah." Rita brushed her denials aside. "Do you know what you want for lunch?"

"No." She looked around, her gaze sweeping the lunch crowd scattered at the tiny white tables shaded by green-and-white striped umbrellas. "Aren't we going to wait for Maria? Weren't the three of us going to have lunch together?"

"Well, we were," Rita said. "But Maria's got some weird flu bug or something. Can't keep anything down lately."

"Oh, I'm sorry."

"She'll live." Rita set her menu down and folded her hands on the table in front of her. "Besides, without her here, I can ask more questions."

"Swell."

Questions Daisy couldn't answer. Questions she really didn't want to even think about.

The waiter stepped up to their table, notepad in hand and a surly expression on his face. Professionally speaking, Daisy thought he deserved a talking to. If any of the wait staff at Antonio's greeted customers like that, they would find themselves out on the street looking for a new job.

"I'll have the club sandwich and tea," Rita said.

"Tuna and a diet soda, please," Daisy ordered.

"Right." He snatched the menus up, turned on his heel and marched off.

"Charming," Daisy muttered.

"Oh no," Rita said, smiling. "You're not going to get me off track by talking about a *waiter,* for God's sake."

"You're on the wrong track already," Daisy said, wincing a little from the dismissive way Rita had said the word *waiter*. After all, she was a waitress. And a darned good one. Actually, with her maternity leave almost up, she'd be heading back to Antonio's soon. Still, even the best waitress probably wouldn't make much of an impression on the Barone family. Single mother, working waitress… Oh yeah, Daisy was sure the Barones would consider her prime "wife" material for Alex.

Wife?

Where had that come from?

But she couldn't lie to herself, could she?

Not when she knew all about the idle fantasies and daydreams she sometimes entertained. Like the one where Alex was her husband and Angel's daddy, and they lived happily ever after in a sweet little cottage with a real English garden in the yard? But as that daydream swam to the surface of her mind, it splintered in the too-bright light of reality.

Daisy reached for her water glass and reminded herself that she wasn't silly enough to believe fairy tales were real or that dreams could come true.

"See, I don't think I am," Rita said softly. "I think my big brother's in love with you."

Rule number one, Daisy told herself later, *never* be taking a drink of water when someone says something foolish.

As she choked and gagged and fought for air, Rita jumped out of her chair, ran around the table and gave her a couple of whopping big slaps on the back. When the pain of that equaled the panic of not being able to breathe, Daisy raised one hand in surrender. At last, though, the choking eased, and after she took a long, unsteady breath, she looked at the other woman and said, "You're nuts."

"Funny," Rita murmured as she sat down again and draped her napkin across her lap. "That's just what Alex said."

"You told *him* your suspicions?"

"It's not like he doesn't know already."

"This is ridiculous." Flustered, torn between wanting to believe and wanting to forget this whole conversation had ever happened, Daisy snapped, "He's just being nice. He doesn't love me."

"Honey," Rita said softly, with a small shake of her head, "nobody's that nice. There's more to it than that. Alex loves you."

"He's fond of the baby, that's all," she argued, shooting one quick glance at her sleeping daughter.

"Oh, sure he is. He's crazy about Angel. But he's also in love with her mother. And I didn't think he'd ever love anyone again."

Whatever she'd been about to say completely slipped Daisy's mind as she focused on one word. "Again?"

A busboy brought their drinks, and Rita smiled her thanks and waited until he'd left again before continuing. "He was engaged. A couple of years ago."

"Engaged."

Rita shuddered. "Awful woman."

"Engaged." One part of Daisy's mind knew she sounded like a parrot, but she just couldn't seem to help it. He'd been engaged to marry someone. He'd loved another woman enough to ask her to marry him. And Daisy was willing to bet he hadn't settled for telling *her* that he "wanted" her.

"She broke their engagement just a week or so before the wedding."

"That's terrible."

"I know. Alex was hurt. And rightly so. But also," Rita said thoughtfully, "I think it burned him. Turned him off love. I honestly never thought he'd fall again."

"He hasn't."

"Uh-huh."

"Really."

Rita just smiled, and Daisy thought she'd never noticed before how annoying a smile could be.

"I know my brother," Rita said. "And whatever he thinks, he's in love."

"Are all of you Barones mind readers?"

"What?"

Really shaken now, all Daisy could think was to get away. To get far away to somewhere quiet so she could think. Tiny ripples of panic surged and receded in the pit of her stomach. She'd like to believe Rita, but she just couldn't risk it. Not now. Not with Angel to think about. She'd believed in Jeff, trusted him. And she'd ended up alone and pregnant.

She wasn't about to set herself up for heartbreak again.

Heck, everyone made mistakes. But the least a person could do was to try to make some new ones.

"Daisy, don't go—"

"I'm sorry, I—" Standing up, she came face-to-face with the surly waiter, who'd finally deigned to appear with their lunches.

"Are you leaving?" he demanded, smacking her plate down onto the table with enough carelessness that some of the fresh fruit tumbled off the plate onto the tabletop and from there to the ground.

"Yes, I am," Daisy said. Then, before she could stop herself, she went on. "And you know, you should put more enthusiasm into your job or simply quit. People don't want to be served by someone who's glowering at them."

He opened his mouth to speak, but she cut him off.

"Good manners don't cost a thing, and you might actually see an increase in your tips if you tried using a few." Then she nodded at Rita, grabbed the stroller handle and pushed her daughter off down the street.

She never heard the smattering of applause from the other patrons, and missed completely the smile Rita sent after her.

"Who does she think she is?" the waiter grumbled.

"A very smart woman," Rita snapped, and tossed a twenty-dollar bill onto the table before she left. She had a phone call to make.

Eleven

The next day Alex stood on Huntington Avenue, staring up at the five-story chrome-and-glass building that was the headquarters of Baronessa Gelati. In front of the impressive building were well-tended gardens, with every kind of flower imaginable bursting with scent and color. Several trees shaded the sidewalk and the entryway to the building, giving the whole place a casual, welcoming air.

But there was nothing at all casual about Baronessa Gelati. His family had built a solid reputation by being the best. And being the best required work. Lots of it.

He'd done his share of that work growing up. All

of his brothers and sisters had served their time in the gelateria in the North End or running errands here at the headquarters. And most of them had decided to join the family business.

But Alex had known from the time he was a kid that a nine-to-five life just wasn't for him. He'd wanted adventure. He'd wanted to travel the world. To do something important with his life.

And in the military, he'd found his place.

Still, he was Barone enough to feel a quick surge of pride as he looked at what his family had accomplished. Stuffing his hands into his pockets, he started up the walkway and entered the building as the automatic doors swished open in silent welcome.

The heels of his worn, brown leather boots clicked noisily against the marble floor as he crossed the foyer. He barely glanced at the framed photos, awards and plaques dotting the walls. He didn't have to. He'd helped hang most of them. It was a picture gallery explaining the history of Baronessa, and as a Barone, he already knew the story inside out. He waved one hand at the man sitting behind the reception desk and headed for the elevators.

When a door opened, he stepped inside and punched the button for the fifth floor. Then he leaned back against the wall, folded his arms across his chest and watched the light dance across the floor numbers as the elevator rose.

And in those few minutes, a thousand thoughts

catapulted through his mind. Most of them were just rehashing what he'd been thinking about since talking to Mike the day before.

Hell.

What he'd been thinking about since walking into Antonio's for dinner six weeks ago.

Daisy.

She haunted his dreams at night and dominated his thoughts during the day. She'd somehow become such a part of his world, he couldn't imagine that world without her in it.

Which was why he'd come here today. Before talking to Daisy, he wanted to tell his family what was going on, what he was feeling. Hell, maybe he was looking for a little encouragement. Someone to tell him that being in love didn't necessarily forebode disaster.

Alex snorted and unfolded himself from his slouched position as the elevator chimed and the door opened. Yeah, he was in great shape. A navy pilot, trusted with a gazillion-dollar jet, counted on to defend his country, and here he stood, wanting someone to tell him that love didn't have to hurt.

A quiet hum of efficiency greeted him as he stalked down the long, carpeted hall toward his father's office. Secretaries and assistants hustled along the corridors, phones rang and some kind of soft, Italian Muzak filtered through the discretely placed wall speakers.

Alex nodded at his father's secretary, who smiled and waved him in. Pushing through the door, Alex paused on the threshold to admire the huge, elegantly appointed office. An antique desk stood directly in front of a floor-to-ceiling window that displayed an awesome view of the city. A hand-carved bar, crowded with dozens of crystal decanters, took up most of one wall, and along another was a cluster of cushy sofas facing each other in a tight circle, as if inviting intimate conversations or friendly business deals.

Two straight-back chairs faced his father's desk and behind it sat the man himself, in a deep-maroon leather chair. Carlo Barone held a phone to his ear, muttered something into the receiver and smiled a greeting to Alex. Motioning him inside, he gave his attention back to the person on the other end of the line, giving Alex a chance to study his father.

At sixty-five, Carlo was still a vigorous, no-nonsense man, from his military-style brush cut to the tips of his gleaming black wingtip shoes. The gray at his temples didn't fool anyone who knew him into thinking he'd slowed down in any way.

While Alex waited, he walked around the room, studying the framed family photos that covered much of the wall space. His brothers and sisters, frozen in time, stared back at him, grinning their childhood smiles and bringing a few wistful smiles from Alex in response.

"Honey," a familiar voice said from the doorway, "I didn't know you were coming into the office today."

He turned to grin at his mother. Moira Reardon Barone was already crossing the room, arms open for a hug. She was a tall, elegant woman, with her Irish red hair styled to perfection. At the moment her beautiful green eyes were practically dancing with pleasure.

"Hi, Mom." Alex grabbed her in a tight hug and just for the hell of it lifted her off her feet, until she slapped at his shoulders and giggled like a girl.

"Put me down, you hooligan."

He did, setting her on her feet just as his father hung up the phone and came around his desk to greet him. "Alex! Glad you came by. We've got a little excitement planned for today. The winner of the contest will be announced shortly."

"I can't stay," he said quickly, knowing that every time he came by the office, his father hoped to convince him to resign his commission and join the family firm.

Carlo's bushy black eyebrows drew together briefly in a frown of disappointment, but just as quickly relaxed again. "Well, then, what's up?"

"I think I know," Moira said, staring up at her son with a thoughtful smile on her face. "Rita called me yesterday."

Carlo snorted and moved to the bar. "You talk to

all of the kids every day. What's so special about this one phone call?''

Moira sighed and shook her head at her husband. ''I tried to tell you last night, but you were too busy on the phone to listen.''

Carlo handed her a glass of white wine, his son a cold beer and then, as he led the way to the conversation area, paused long enough to give his wife a loud, smacking kiss on the cheek. ''I was busy lining up western distributors.''

She smiled at him fondly, sent Alex a speculative look and said, ''There are some things more important than business, Carlo.''

Alex frowned, but sat down opposite his parents. Naturally, the two older Barones took their usual positions—side by side. As they had throughout all the years of their marriage, they presented a united front. They'd managed eight children and a growing business by drawing together and holding on tight.

It was the kind of relationship every Barone child had always wanted for his or her own.

''So—'' Carlo nodded at his son while he took a sip of Scotch ''—do you have any idea what she's talking about?''

''No, but—''

His mother interrupted him. ''My guess is he's here to talk about the new woman in his life.''

Carlo brightened. The man was a romantic at

heart. But then, most Italian men were, Alex thought.

"Who is she? When do we meet her?" Carlo turned and looked at his wife. "Why didn't you tell me?"

"I tried, remember? Western distributors?" Moira shifted a glance toward her son and tried to read his expression. But Alex had never been an easy one to figure out. He kept his feelings to himself, while most of her children wore their emotions on their sleeves. And because he buried his hurts and his triumphs deep inside, Alex was the one who was most easily hurt—and the least likely to look for help.

Knowing how badly the breakup of his engagement had torn at him made Moira all the more determined to see that he was more careful in love this time around. It didn't matter to her that Rita had sung Daisy's praises. All that counted here was her son.

"Look," Alex said, setting his beer down on the low, cherry wood cocktail table in front of him. "I just came by to tell you that…well, yeah. About Daisy." Apparently though, he didn't have to tell them about her. Rita had already stepped in and told them everything.

"Daisy, is it?" Carlo practically beamed. "Is she Italian?"

"No. Her last name's Cusak."

"She's a waitress at Antonio's," Moira added.

"Antonio's?" The elder Barone stiffened slightly, then relaxed again. "Doesn't matter." He waved a hand, then frowned when the phone on his desk rang shrilly. He stood up and moved toward it, calling back over his shoulder, "As long as you love her, that's good enough for me."

But he hadn't said he loved her, Alex thought. He hadn't even *thought* it. Oh, he'd admitted to himself that he cared about Daisy. And God knew, he *wanted* her so badly he'd been walking around in pain for weeks now. But love? He didn't know. Reaching for his beer again, he studied the label as though it contained the answers to every one of the questions rushing through his brain. But there were no answers there. Hell, he was in deep trouble.

"Alex," his mother said softly, reaching across the table to lay one hand on his arm.

He looked up into the green eyes that he'd trusted all of his life and found concern written there. Not surprising. Moira Reardon Barone had always been able to connect with her children, to know which of them needed a hug or a swift kick in the rear.

"Rita told me all about you and Daisy. And the baby, as well."

"Rita should keep her nose out of it."

"She loves you."

"She's a buttinsky."

"True," his mother allowed with a smile. "But she does love you. As do I."

"I know that."

"And if you love Daisy, I'm happy for you."

"I—"

"But," Moira said, cutting him off before he could say anything more, "I want you to think about something, too."

He sucked in a deep breath, blew it out in a rush and asked, "What?"

"I know how attached you've become to Daisy's baby—"

"Rita really shot her mouth off, didn't she?"

His mother smiled, that patient, understanding smile that had always told him she saw far too much for him to try to get away with anything.

"Yes, she did. But you told us about the baby that first night, remember? How you and the girls had helped Daisy deliver?"

"Yeah, I remember."

"That kind of emotional connection is a very strong one. It can color your emotions, cloud the issues."

He ground his teeth together. "This isn't just about the baby, Mom."

"I'm sure it's not. But what I want you to think about now," his mother said, "is just this. Is it Daisy you love? Or is it the idea of having a family of your own that's drawing you?" She pulled her hand back and shook her head. "Don't get that stubborn look on your face. It's an honest question. And one you have to consider carefully. For both your own sake and Daisy's. Not to mention the child's."

Alex jumped to his feet and looked down at her. Moira wasn't deterred. She'd been dealing with Italian tempers for a long time now. And coming from a family of Irishmen every bit as stubborn as the Barones, she'd long ago learned to stand her ground.

"If what you're feeling isn't really love, Alex, you'll not only be cheating yourself, but cheating Daisy out of what everyone has a right to expect."

He scraped one hand across his face. Reasonable. Her argument was perfectly reasonable. There was just one problem. "And how am I supposed to know if it's love? I thought I was in love the last time. But when she left me, I got over it."

Moira shook her head, stood up and gave her son a brief, hard hug before stepping back with a smile. "There's no signpost, Alex. No bolt of lightning. No fireworks. There's just a *knowing,* deep inside you. In your heart. Your soul. If it's love, you'll know it's there."

"And if I don't?"

"Then that's your answer, isn't it?"

"I...care for her, Mom." A weak word, *care.* It didn't come close to describing what he felt for Daisy. For Angel. It didn't explain the wild fantasies and the silly daydreams that had become a part of his life over the last several weeks.

"I'm sure you do," Moira said softly. "But the question is, how *much* do you care?"

Before he could answer, his father hung up the phone and called out, "Moira! We've got our contest winner! It's a young woman named…" He checked his notes "…Holly Fitzgerald."

Moira grinned at her husband. "Up the Irish."

A few hours later, Daisy answered the door with a heavy heart. She didn't know what to do anymore. What to think. Alex was just…Alex. A part of her life now. The star of her dreams. The hero of her fantasies.

And yet, there was so much separating them. So much standing in the way of them ever finding a life together.

She opened the door and her breath caught in her throat as she stared up into his dark brown eyes. For the rest of her life, even if she never saw him again, she would be able to close her eyes and remember his. The warmth. The heat of his stare. The flash of desire that quickened in their depths.

He ran one hand across the side of his head, glanced back down the empty hallway, then shifted his gaze to her. "Daisy, I wanted to see you. I need to talk to you about something."

Goodbye, she thought. He hadn't said the word,

but it was drifting in the air between them. Her heart ached and a small voice in the back of her mind wept for the end of what had been a lovely dream.

"Sure." She forced herself to step back, waving him inside. Better to get this over with, she told herself, lifting her chin bravely, as if she expected to take a solid blow on the tip of it.

She'd known for weeks this was coming. Had told herself to prepare for it. And yet now that it was here, pain welled up inside her until she could hardly breathe. She wanted to jump into his arms and kiss him. Feel his arms come around her. She wanted to tell him that she'd been to the doctor. That he'd given her the okay to resume her normal life.

She wanted to ask Alex to make love to her. To touch her and be inside her. To fill her with his body until she would never really be alone again.

But the words died, unuttered. She couldn't do it. Couldn't make love with him and then let him go. The pain of knowing what she would never have again would be too much to live with. Better to walk away before finding the magic she knew existed in the circle of his arms.

He walked across the small living room, and the strength of his presence seemed to fill the place until it felt no bigger than a closet. Daisy pulled in a slow, deep breath and fought for calm as her gaze drifted over him. She took in his long legs encased in worn, faded denim, his scarred boots that only made him taller. He wore a dark red open-collared shirt that tantalized her by offering a peek at a small V of his chest. His eyes were dark and troubled, and Daisy knew that whatever he was about to say, she wasn't going to like it.

"Where's Angel?" he asked, throwing her off guard.

"She's asleep," Daisy said, and wished the baby were here—a small, warm body to cling to. Then, instantly, she was ashamed of herself for wanting to hide behind her own child.

"Oh." He reached up and viciously rubbed the back of his neck. "I was hoping to see her before—" He stopped and stared at Daisy.

"Before you left?" she finished for him, silently congratulating herself on being able to say the words without her voice breaking.

He looked miserable. And if she wasn't mistaken, there was just a hint of sympathy in his eyes. Well, she didn't want his pity. Didn't want him feeling sorry for her. She'd be fine. She'd survived Jeff's abandonment and she'd get through this, too.

She was used to making do on her own. Used to counting on no one but herself. And though it killed her to realize her greatest fears were coming true— he really *was* walking away from her—she'd make out all right. Just as she always had.

Alex crossed the room in three long strides and suddenly he was there. Beside her.

"I don't want to go, Daisy."

She felt the heat of his hands on her bare arms and wished she wasn't wearing a short-sleeved shirt. But even as she thought it, she knew a thick sweater and a parka wouldn't be enough to keep her from feeling his touch right down to her bones.

Still, she steeled herself against the effect he had on her and forced herself to step back, out of his grasp, away from the hard, solid strength of him.

"Of course you don't," she said, keeping in her voice a lightness she wasn't feeling. "You're a nice man. But we both knew that you'd be leaving. Going back to the navy."

"Not yet."

"What?"

"I still have ten days of leave. I'm just going to my family's place in Harwichport for a few days."

Daisy crossed her arms in front of her chest and held on tightly. She knew what he was doing. He might think he wasn't leaving her yet, but that's exactly what this was. He was pulling away gently. Trying to make his inevitable goodbye easier on her. That was impossible, though. Because knowing he was leaving had finally made her realize a single hard truth.

She loved Alex Barone.

And she was going to lose him.

Misery was lurking just out of sight, but was already closing in. But at least she could hang on to her pride. She wouldn't let him know she loved him. Wouldn't let on that his leaving was killing her.

Because if she did, and he turned his back and walked away from her love—as Jeff once had—the pain would be unbearable. Better to keep her feelings to herself and make him believe that she was fine with his going.

"Of course you want to visit with your family before you ship out," she said, and was silently proud of herself for being so strong.

"I'll be back in a few days."

"I'll be here," she quipped, and gave him a smile that cost every ounce of her strength. Yes, she'd be here. Angel would be here. But Daisy wasn't expecting to ever see Alex here again.

He'd go to his family. Be back in his world. And soon enough, Daisy and her child would slip to the rear of his mind, and in no time at all, they'd be nothing more than a pleasant, if vague, memory.

And he'd never know he'd left her heart in splinters.

Twelve

Four days later, Alex was going out of his mind.

He loved his family, but all he could think about was Daisy. Always before when he'd come home to Boston on leave, he'd spent every moment he could with his brothers, his sisters, his parents. He'd wanted to saturate himself with the love and strength of the Barones.

Now, though, his heart just wasn't in it.

He wondered if she was thinking about him. If she missed him, if she was wishing he'd come back—or if she was just glad to be rid of him. And Angel, the tiny baby who'd captured his heart within moments of her birth. Had she grown? Had she changed? Was she aware enough to even notice he was gone from her life? As she grew up, would she ever know that he'd been there at her beginning? That he'd loved her as much as any father could?

"No." Alex spat the word out, to hear how it sounded. To see how it felt. And the instant he did, he knew the plain simple truth.

Shaking his head, he stared out the window of the room that had been his as a boy. Looking past his own reflection, he focused on the distance—toward Boston and Daisy. Where his heart was.

"I love her." So simple. So easy. And now that the words were said, admitted to, he felt a swell of pleasure so deep and rich, it shook him right down to his soul.

"You're sure?"

He turned around to find his mother standing in the open doorway, smiling.

"Yeah," he said, grinning in response. "I'm sure."

"Then why are you still here?" she asked.

"Because I'm an idiot," he answered, already moving for the door.

"Well, that's all right, then," his mother told him. "Women are used to dealing with and *forgiving* idiots."

"I hope you're right."

"I usually am," she said. "Just ask your father."

Alex laughed and started past her, hurrying down

the hall toward the staircase. Now that the decision was made, he couldn't wait another minute to find Daisy. To tell her that he loved her. To ask her to marry him and *insist* that she say yes.

"I'm looking forward to meeting Daisy," his mother called after him, "and my new granddaughter!"

Daisy tried to keep her mind on work.

It wasn't easy, though. Despite the heavy crowd at Antonio's, her thoughts kept drifting. It was good to be back at work, however. Heaven knew it was better than sitting in her apartment doing nothing but moping about Alex. At least here she was too busy to mope *all* the time.

There was one bright spot in all this. Her friend Joan and she had arranged to work different shifts, so Joan was watching Angel while Daisy worked. At least she was spared having to worry about her baby while she tried to get on with her life.

When the hostess seated a man at one of Daisy's empty tables, she was pleased. One more customer to keep her mind busy, she thought. Until she went to take his order and was caught by Alex's steady gaze.

Her heart jumped in her chest, and it was suddenly hard to breathe. "What are you doing here?"

"I went to your apartment. Joan told me you were working tonight."

"But why are you here?"

"For dinner."

"Dinner?"

"To start."

Daisy looked at him, drinking in the sight of him, and told herself that this didn't mean anything. The fact that he was back when she'd never expected to see him again was just a blip. A painful one.

"Alex…"

"I'd like the chicken parmigiana, please. And coffee."

"Fine." She nodded and snatched up the menu. If he could do this, so could she. Just business. She'd wait on him, then he would leave and hopefully stay the heck away—at least until she could get over him. That shouldn't take more than ten or twenty years.

The next couple of hours flew by. With every step she took, she felt Alex's gaze on her. She went hot and cold every few seconds and made more mistakes with her customers' orders than she had on her first night as a waitress. When her shift was over, she went to his table to take his check and spotted the fifty-dollar bill he was leaving on a twenty-five dollar tab.

"I don't want your money, Alex," she said tightly, leaving it right where it lay. Then she turned and stormed through the restaurant.

Alex was just a step or two behind her and caught

up with her right outside. Grabbing her upper arm, he pulled her around to face him.

"Why are you doing this to me?" She reached up to shove her hair back from her face. "Why did you come back?"

"I missed you," he said, and those three little words slipped into her heart and eased away the ache that seemed to have always been with her.

"Alex…" Daisy looked up at him, trying to ignore the feel of his hand on her skin.

"I had to see you."

"It's not a good idea."

"It's the only good idea I've had in the last five days."

"Don't do this to me. To us."

"That's just it," he murmured. "There *is* an us, Daisy. Whether we planned it or not."

He skimmed the tips of his fingers along the line of her cheek. She shivered. Daisy's heart squeezed just a little bit tighter and she wondered what its breaking point was.

Damp summer heat crowded around them, pushing them together, drawing them closer. She felt as though she couldn't breathe, and worse, Daisy didn't *want* to breathe. She didn't need air when she could look into Alex's eyes and feel the power of his soul reaching into hers.

"What now?" she managed to ask, despite the hard knot of need lodged in her throat.

Alex leaned in, kissed her hard and long and deeply, then reared back, gave her a quick grin and said, "Your place. *Now.*"

She didn't remember the cab ride.

City traffic and the summer crowds dissolved into a colorful blur beyond the windows as Alex's hands moved over her body. His clever fingers slipped beneath the hem of her skirt, slid up her thigh and stroked her center until even with the flimsy silk barrier of her panties protecting her, Daisy squirmed on the frayed leather seat. She didn't know how it had happened. How she'd gone from missing him to being fondled in the back seat of a cab. But she told herself not to question it. To simply accept the moment. To glory in the magic that was Alex.

He couldn't touch her enough. Couldn't feel her enough. Trapped in the back of a cab, streaming through downtown Boston, he indulged himself and tortured both of them. How could he ever have thought he could leave her? How could he have doubted what he'd found with her? And how would he convince her to be with him forever?

The cab jerked to a stop outside her apartment building, and briefly, Alex considered telling the driver to just keep going. To keep driving so that he wouldn't have to stop touching her. But in the next instant, reality crashed through his brain, reminding

him that he'd have to get her out of the damn cab
to get her out of her damn clothes.

Alex tossed the driver a handful of bills, exited
the taxi and took Daisy's hand to help her out. In
the soft glow of the streetlight, her face was flushed,
her eyes wide and her mouth soft and delectable.
They practically ran into the building, and on the
long elevator ride, Daisy turned into his arms and
kissed him until Alex was pretty sure he felt his
blood boil. When the door opened, they hurried
down the long, ugly hallway, and Daisy fumbled for
her key.

"Hurry."

"I'm trying."

The door flew open and Joan took a long look at
them. Then, grinning, she snatched up her purse,
saying, "Angel's sound asleep. Have a good night."
She left, shutting the door behind her. In the next
instant, Alex was on Daisy.

Hands.

Everywhere.

He touched her and she went up in flames.

She sighed and his body went rock hard and
ready.

Daisy's brain shut down. She didn't want to think,
didn't want to worry about tomorrow. All she
wanted was now. Tonight. And the unrelenting pleasure of Alex's hands on her skin. She'd thought before that the only way to deal with not having him

in her life was to never fully experience having him in her body. But now she knew that if she never had another moment with him, she wanted—*needed* this one.

In seconds, he'd stripped her uniform blouse off her shoulders and down her arms. Her skin chilled in the air, but one look from his eyes and she was on fire again.

"Daisy, you're killin' me," he muttered, sliding his hands over her shoulders and down her chest to the front clasp of her bra.

"Oh," she said with a sigh, "not yet."

Quickly, they tore at each other's clothes. Six long weeks had built to this moment, and they couldn't get naked fast enough. Skirt, pants, shirts, bra littered the floor, and when there was nothing left between them, Alex scooped her up in his arms and carried her into the bedroom.

He laid her down on the quilt-covered mattress in a splash of moonlight. The pale shimmer of light dusted her hair with silver and made her skin gleam like fine porcelain. But she was warm and soft, and as he lay down beside her, she turned into his arms and melded her body to his. Hard to soft, heat to heat, they brushed against each other, fanning the flames within. His hands moved over her, skimming her curves, learning every line. She shivered when he bent his head to take one of her nipples into his mouth, and nearly came off the bed as he suck-led her.

"Alex, please. I need…I need…"

"We both need, Daisy," he whispered, his breath dusting her skin.

Her fingers clutched at his shoulders, then scraped down his back, her short, neat nails dragging at his skin as he took her higher. Daisy arched into him, silently pleading for more. Another kiss. Another swirl of his tongue. Another deep touch, as his fingers found her heated core and stroked her into a kind of madness. While his mouth teased her, tormented her, his fingers played a game of their own, dipping into her warmth and sliding back out again. His thumb continued to caress the small, rigid bead of her sex until she twisted and writhed beneath him in a futile quest to find ease.

Awash with color and sensation, Daisy's mind raced, while her body hummed with electrical pulse beats of excitement. Her hands moved over him, tracing the line of his spine, down to the curve of his rear, then back up and around, to smooth across his muscled chest and down his abdomen. She curled her fingers around the hard length of him and smiled when he hissed in a breath. He was no more immune to her touch than she was to his. And that snippet of power urged her onward.

She stroked him, caressed him, smoothing his hardened flesh until he growled low in his throat, tore his mouth from her breast and glared down at her. "If you keep touching me like that, this is going to be over a hell of a lot faster than I'd planned."

"I want you inside me," she said, tightening her grip just enough to show him how serious she was. "Now, Alex. Be in me. Be deep within me."

Alex didn't need any more urging. Every cell in his body wanted the same damn thing. And after six long weeks of want, maybe slow and easy wasn't the way to go, anyway. He shifted, positioning himself between her thighs, and when she lifted her hips in silent invitation, he couldn't wait another minute.

Slowly, carefully, he entered her. Watching her face, terrified that he might hurt her, he pushed his body into hers and didn't release the breath he was holding until he was buried within her heat and she smiled at him.

"I'm not fragile," she whispered, reaching up to him. "I won't break."

"I don't want to hurt you."

"The only way you can do that now is to stop."

"Not a chance, baby."

Levering himself atop her, he rocked his hips, claiming her as completely as he could. She moved with him, arching into his every thrust, hooking her legs around his waist and pulling him deeper, closer, until he wasn't sure where his body ended and hers began. And it didn't matter.

All that counted now was that he'd found the

place he belonged. At last, he'd found the home he'd been born to find. And it was here. Inside Daisy. In her body. Her heart.

He bent his head to take her mouth with his, parting her lips, tasting her sighs. When the first ripple of satisfaction coursed through her, he deepened the kiss further, swallowing her moans and tucking them away inside him.

Daisy held on to him and kissed him desperately, wildly, responding to his urgency, his wildness with an eagerness she'd never known before. He was everything. Everything she'd ever hoped for and dreamed of. In his arms, she felt magic shatter within her, and she rode the crest of tiny, soul-splintering explosions and knew she would never be the same again. As he gave her all that he was, she cradled him in her arms, and together they raced toward completion.

Five minutes, an hour, heck, an eternity later, Daisy opened her eyes and stared blindly at the ceiling. At least she guessed it was the ceiling, though how she could see the stars was a little puzzling.

With Alex still draped across her body, still locked inside her, she took a shallow breath and committed to memory the feel of his weight pressing her into the bed. She wanted to remember everything. To savor every touch, every breath.

Because when he was gone, it would be all she had left.

"I love you," he said, his words muffled against her throat.

Daisy stilled, her heart stopped dead in her chest and she wasn't sure she could breathe. But as much as she wanted to hear him say those words and mean them, a part of her knew he'd only said them in reaction to what they'd just shared. So rather than respond, she asked, "When do you have to ship out?"

He lifted his head and looked down at her, confusion clear in his eyes. "Less than a week. Did you hear me?"

"I'll miss you," she said, and lifted one hand to cup his cheek. Her thumb stroked his jaw, which was bristly with whisker stubble.

Scowling now, he propped himself up on his elbow, and with his free hand, captured her fingers in a tight grip. "Didn't you hear me? I said *I love you.*"

"Yes, I heard you," she answered, then tore her gaze from his, looking anywhere but into those dark brown eyes. A yawning black hole opened up inside her, though she managed to keep her voice even as she said, "But we both know you didn't mean it."

"Is that right?" His voice sounded tight, cold and hard. "Just what did I mean, then?"

"You meant the sex was good."

"No, the sex was great. I said I love you."

"Alex, don't do this." She pushed at his chest in

a ridiculous attempt to shove his much bigger body off of hers. She chanced a look into his eyes and almost instantly wished she hadn't. There was no spark of desire there now. Just confusion. And anger.

He made no move to get off her. Instead, he shifted, rising up onto his knees, but keeping her with him, their bodies locked together. She was pinned onto his lap like a butterfly trapped under glass. Grasping her hips, he held her down when she would have scooted off him.

"Are you trying to tell me you don't love me?" he demanded. "'Cause if that's what you're up to, I don't buy it."

"I didn't say that," she snapped, tossing her hair out of her eyes and giving escape one more try. Pointless. His hands held her tightly and the hard, rigid length of him was pushed so deeply inside her, she wasn't going anywhere. Slapping her hands down onto his shoulders, she forced herself to meet his gaze squarely. "What I feel for you doesn't really matter."

"Matters a hell of a lot to me," he countered.

"You're leaving and I—"

"You what?"

"I'm staying."

He sighed heavily. "Look, I know being a navy wife won't be easy, but—"

"A *wife?*" She reared back and stared at him as if he'd lost his mind.

"Well, what did you think I was talking about?"

"You're crazy," she said, and tried to scoot off him again. But all she managed to do was send tiny ribbons of heat winding throughout her body. He rocked into her, tripling the effect until her eyes rolled in her head and she clung to him just to keep her balance.

"I want you to marry me," Alex said, and fought back a groan as she moved on him, taking him deeper within.

"You don't want to marry me."

"Why don't I?" Stop moving, he thought, but he didn't say it because he didn't really want her to stop moving.

"Because you're a *Barone*. I'm a *waitress*."

"So?"

"It wouldn't work. I just don't—"

"You're a waitress. My family makes ice cream," he said, his anger fading as he realized that she was trying to protect him from himself. "Seems like a perfect match to me."

"Alex, you don't know what you're saying."

"I always say what I mean, Daisy. You know that by now."

"Yes, but—"

"But nothing. Just answer one question. Do you love me?"

She looked at him, her gaze soft and wide and filled with a renewed pulse of desire that tore at him. He slid his hands from her hips up to her breasts and cupped them gently, kneading her nipples until she finally gasped, "Yes. Yes, I do love you. I tried not to but—"

"Then marry me," he whispered, lowering his head to kiss first one rigid nipple, then the other. "Marry me and put me out of my misery."

Daisy shook her head, trying desperately to think. To keep her brain functioning despite what he was doing to her. "Angel," she said. "I have a daughter and—"

He lifted his head, reached up and cradled her face between his palms. "*We* have a daughter." He said the words firmly, so there would never be a mistake about it. "I've loved her from the moment she was born. She's the child of my heart, Daisy, and if it's all right with you, as soon as we're married, I'll start the adoption process to make her mine legally, too."

Tears filled her eyes and his image blurred. Moonlight swam around them like a thick, silver fog and she knew that she would never forget this night. "Alex—"

But whatever she would have said was lost when they heard the baby whimper. This time when Daisy moved off of him, he let her go. She left the room and went into the nursery they'd created together, and Alex was right behind her.

Angel lay in her bed, sound asleep and making the tiny mewling noises that tore at every parent's heart. Daisy reached down and stroked her daughter's back, whispering soft assurances that calmed the child and sent her back into a dreamless sleep.

Alex wrapped his arms around the woman he loved and watched the child that had brought them together. In the soft light of the lamp, he stared into blue eyes that held the only world he cared about.

"Marry me, Daisy. Love me. Make a family with me."

She looked up at him and knew she was lost. She'd been lost from the moment he'd first stepped into Antonio's. Her life had changed that one, miraculous night and she knew that she'd been given a great gift. How foolish she would be to turn it down.

"Yes, Alex. I will marry you. And I will love you as long as I live."

He kissed her gently, softly, tenderly, with a promise of tomorrow as he led her back to her bedroom. And this time, when he laid her down on the bed and stretched out beside her, his heart was full. She was his love. His life. And he silently thanked whatever Fate had sent her to him.

Sliding down the length of her body, he kissed

her, adored her and caressed her skin until she tingled with anticipation.

"Kiss me, Alex," she said softly, reaching for him.

He smiled at her and said, "I plan to," just before he scooped his hands beneath her bottom and lifted her off the mattress. Lowering his head, he covered her with his mouth, giving her a kiss of another sort. An intimate touch of tongue and lips. He tasted and savored and suckled, pushing her higher than she'd been before. Sending her to places she'd only dreamed existed.

Daisy closed her eyes, then opened them wide again, determined to watch him as he took her. His tongue stroked her center in a damp kiss that sent goose bumps racing along her spine. His strong fingers kneaded her behind, and as he worked her body, she gave herself up to the sensations coursing through her.

She'd found a lover.

She'd found a husband.

And a father for Angel.

And more, she'd found the missing piece of her own heart. Right there, in a pair of warm brown eyes.

Deep within, a chain reaction began. Sensation piled on top of sensation until she quivered in his grasp and heard herself beg, "Take me, Alex. Be inside me again when it happens."

Instantly, he set her down and moved to claim her as his own. He entered her with a long, slow thrust that she swore later had touched her soul. And when the skyrockets exploded, they clung together and drifted through the stars.

Epilogue

Three days later

It was a small, hurried wedding. With a special license and the blessings of the Barones, Alex and Daisy were married in Moira's garden.

Tiny Angel wailed through most of the ceremony, but no one seemed to mind. The day was just too perfect.

And as Alex slipped the simple gold band onto Daisy's finger, she smiled into his eyes. Yes, he would be leaving in two days. But once he'd been assigned quarters at whatever base he was being sent to, she and Angel would be following him.

Until then, she would have her new family around her and a golden ring of promise to keep her warm.

"You may kiss the bride," the minister said, a broad smile on his face.

"Now that's the best idea I've heard all day," Alex told him, and pulled Daisy close.

She wrapped her arms around his neck and glanced at Rita, who was trying desperately to quiet the baby. Then, smiling, Daisy looked back at her new husband. "I think your daughter wants a kiss, too."

He grinned, and Daisy wondered if her toes would always curl when he smiled at her like that.

"She'll have to wait her turn," he murmured, so only she could hear. "Right now it's her mama I'm interested in."

"Then kiss me, sailor."

"Aye-aye, Mrs. Barone."

As his lips closed over hers, Daisy felt her heart swell until it nearly choked her. She'd found everything she'd ever dreamed of, right here in Alex's arms. No matter where they lived, or how many places the navy sent them, she knew without a doubt that *home* would always be where her hero was.

* * * * *

DYNASTIES: THE BARONES
continues....
*Turn the page for a bonus look at
what's in store for you in the next
Barones book
—only from Silhouette Desire!*
*1520 CINDERELLA'S MILLIONAIRE
by Katherine Garbera
July 2003*

One

There were times when it didn't pay to be part of a big Italian family, Joseph Barone thought as he listened to his sister Gina give him last-minute instructions on how to handle the press today. She was the PR person, and in his opinion the one who should be escorting the contest winner—Holly Fitzgerald—around. But Gina and Flint thought it would be better if an executive did the honors. And somehow he was the only one who would get up at five in the morning to handle this latest volley in Baronessa's PR plan.

"If anyone brings up the passion fruit gelato debacle, acknowledge that it was a mistake and one that Baronessa won't make again. Then use the fact sheet I gave you on the new flavor.''

''Got it,'' he said.

Gina smiled at him. ''Thanks for doing this.''

''As if I had any choice.'' Joe had tried arguing, but it was hard to win with his mother or sisters. Italian women never fought fair, and in the end guilt and familial duty had won out.

Joe watched his sister walk away. Gina had changed in the last few months since her marriage to Flint Kingman. But then, finding the love of your life could do that to a person.

He'd changed after he'd met Mary. And then changed again after she'd died. But some things were better left in the past, and Mary was one of them.

''Here she is,'' Gina said, entering the conference room with another woman.

Joe's breath caught in his chest. The woman walking toward him bore an uncanny resemblance to his deceased wife. Slim and petite, she had auburn hair that fell in waves around her shoulders. Mary's hair had been shorter, he thought. But her features were similar. Heart-shaped face, full lips and a nose that curved the slightest bit at the end.

Joe prided himself on his resilience. He'd survived things that would have destroyed a lesser man. But the last thing he wanted was to tour the company's headquarters with the doppelgänger of his deceased wife. Gina would just have to do it.

"Holly Fitzgerald, this is my brother and Baronessa's Chief Financial Officer, Joseph Barone."

"Pleased to meet you, Ms. Fitzgerald," Joe said, shaking her hand. It felt soft, small, fragile. Damn. It had been a long time—five years, to be exact—since he'd held a hand that delicate.

"Please call me Holly."

He nodded. He'd survived the crushing grief that followed his wife's death by keeping himself aloof from women, by letting no one but family close to him, and he didn't intend to let this contest winner rock the secure moorings of his world....

*   *   *   *   *

DYNASTIES: THE BARONES

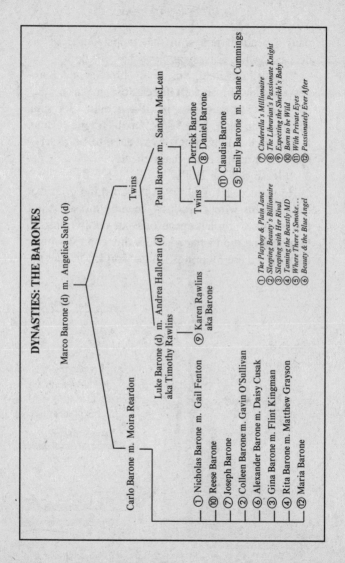

Marco Barone (d) m. Angelica Salvo (d)

Carlo Barone m. Moira Reardon

Luke Barone (d) m. Andrea Halloran (d)
aka Timothy Rawlins

Twins

Paul Barone m. Sandra MacLean

⑨ Karen Rawlins
aka Barone

Twins

Derrick Barone
⑧ Daniel Barone

⑪ Claudia Barone

⑤ Emily Barone m. Shane Cummings

① Nicholas Barone m. Gail Fenton
⑩ Reese Barone
⑦ Joseph Barone
② Colleen Barone m. Gavin O'Sullivan
⑥ Alexander Barone m. Daisy Cusak
③ Gina Barone m. Flint Kingman
④ Rita Barone m. Matthew Grayson
⑫ Maria Barone

① *The Playboy & Plain Jane*
② *Sleeping Beauty's Billionaire*
③ *Sleeping with Her Rival*
④ *Taming the Beastly MD*
⑤ *Where There's Smoke....*
⑥ *Beauty & the Blue Angel*

⑦ *Cinderella's Millionaire*
⑧ *The Librarian's Passionate Knight*
⑨ *Expecting the Sheikh's Baby*
⑩ *Born to be Wild*
⑪ *With Private Eyes*
⑫ *Passionately Ever After*

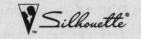

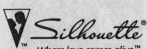

If you enjoyed what you just read,
then we've got an offer you can't resist!

Take 2 bestselling
love stories FREE!

Plus get a FREE surprise gift!

Clip this page and mail it to Silhouette Reader Service™

IN U.S.A.
3010 Walden Ave.
P.O. Box 1867
Buffalo, N.Y. 14240-1867

IN CANADA
P.O. Box 609
Fort Erie, Ontario
L2A 5X3

YES! Please send me 2 free Silhouette Desire® novels and my free surprise gift. After receiving them, if I don't wish to receive anymore, I can return the shipping statement marked cancel. If I don't cancel, I will receive 6 brand-new novels every month, before they're available in stores! In the U.S.A., bill me at the bargain price of $3.57 plus 25¢ shipping and handling per book and applicable sales tax, if any*. In Canada, bill me at the bargain price of $4.24 plus 25¢ shipping and handling per book and applicable taxes**. That's the complete price and a savings of at least 10% off the cover prices—what a great deal! I understand that accepting the 2 free books and gift places me under no obligation ever to buy any books. I can always return a shipment and cancel at any time. Even if I never buy another book from Silhouette, the 2 free books and gift are mine to keep forever.

225 SDN DNUP
326 SDN DNUQ

Name _____ (PLEASE PRINT)

Address _____ Apt.# _____

City _____ State/Prov. _____ Zip/Postal Code _____

* Terms and prices subject to change without notice. Sales tax applicable in N.Y.
** Canadian residents will be charged applicable provincial taxes and GST.
   All orders subject to approval. Offer limited to one per household and not valid to current Silhouette Desire® subscribers.
   ® are registered trademarks of Harlequin Books S.A., used under license.

DES02   ©1998 Harlequin Enterprises Limited

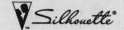

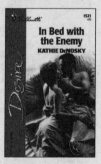
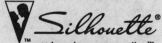

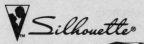

COMING NEXT MONTH

#1519 SCENES OF PASSION—Suzanne Brockmann
Maggie Stanton knew something was missing from her picture-perfect
life, and when she ran into her high school buddy Michael Stone, she
knew just what it was. The former bad boy had grown into a charismatic
man who was everything Maggie had ever dreamed of. But if they were
to have a future together, Maggie would have to learn to trust him.

#1520 CINDERELLA'S MILLIONAIRE—Katherine Garbera
Dynasties: The Barones
Love was the last thing on widower Joseph Barone's mind…until
he was roped into escorting pastry chef Holly Fitzgerald to a media
interview. The brooding millionaire had built an impenetrable wall
around his heart, but delectable Holly was pure temptation. He needed
her—in his bed and in his life—but was he ready to risk his heart again?

#1521 IN BED WITH THE ENEMY—Kathie DeNosky
Lone Star Country Club
ATF agent Cole Yardley didn't believe women belonged in the field,
fighting crime, but then a gun-smuggling investigation brought him and
FBI agent Elise Campbell together. Though he'd intended to ignore Elise,
Cole soon found himself surrendering to the insatiable hunger she stirred
in him.…

#1522 EXPECTING THE COWBOY'S BABY—Charlene Sands
An old flame came roaring back to life when Cassie Munroe went home
for her brother's wedding and ran into Jake Griffin, her high school ex.
The boy who'd broken her heart was gone, and in his place was one
sinfully sexy man. They wound up sharing an unforgettable night of
passion that would change Cassie's life forever, for now she was pregnant
with Jake's baby!

#1523 CHEROKEE DAD—Sheri WhiteFeather
Desperate to keep her nephew safe, Heather Richmond turned to
Michael Elk, the man she'd left behind eighteen months ago. Michael
still touched her soul in a way no other man ever had, and she couldn't
resist the seductive promises in his eyes. She only hoped he would
forgive her once he discovered her secret.…

#1524 THE GENTRYS: CAL—Linda Conrad
When Cal Gentry went home to his family ranch to recover from the
accident that killed his wife, he found Isabella de la Cruz on his doorstep.
The mysterious beauty needed protecting…and soon found a sense of
security in Cal's arms. Then, as things heated up between them, Cal
vowed to convince Isabella to accept not only his protection, but his
heart, as well.

SDCNM0603